The
Red
Button

*A novel that tells what
became of Belle & Scrooge*

Keith Eldred

this is RED
thisis.red

Learn more about the author and the THIS IS RED
project at www.thisis.red

Cover design by Keith Eldred
Cover images used by license from Freepik

Get your
THIS IS RED
starter library
FREE

Sign up for no-spam email updates
and get four Christmas books and
other special offers, all for free

You will find details at the end of this book

Find fresh affection for
A CHRISTMAS CAROL
*with this classic prequel and enjoy
the new holiday tradition of
the Red Button.*

We know they will never marry. They do not.

Belle Endicott's farewell to her fiancé,
Ebenezer Scrooge, has echoed through time:

*"I release you. With a full heart,
for the love of him you once were.
May you be happy in the life you have chosen!"*

Here is the untold story of how the young lovers found
and then lost each other. And how their doomed union
stayed with Scrooge daily and ultimately prepared
the way for his famous redemption.

For my grandmothers,
Hersa Eldred & Irene Lavallee,
strong workers with big hearts

prelude

You know me. I am as close as your heart. No, a little forward and to the right of your heart as you look down. I am a button.

I am nature and art, craft and science. I have the dense grain of wood, the soft mottling of shell, the luxurious gleam of pearl. I am all colors of the rainbow. I am the labor of sculptors, engravers, and engineers. I am perfect cylinders placed in perfect squares within perfect circles. I am as strong as steel, as smooth as glass, as fine as silk.

I exist to serve. I guard modesty, preserve warmth, hold things together.

I am vital. Do I exaggerate? Clearly not. If I go missing, all is undone. Suddenly life is unsuitable and change essential. My loss must be redressed.

I am a paradox: Irreplaceable except by any duplicate. None will do but I—or anyone just like me.

I am the fresh packet of buttons in your sewing box,

the cloth strip of three with clipped threads where there had been a fourth, and I am each fastener who has no mate.

Just now I am the button who is never used as intended. I am never attached to cloth, much less probed by a needle. I never aid closure. In fact, in the story that follows, I witness a lifetime of the opposite.

I am the red button in the pocket of one lonely man, who each night hung me from a hook on his wall using the black cord that he ran through one of my eyes. Three eyes remained open, and one thing I never lacked was the power of perception. Even in the blackness of the man's pockets, there was nothing I could not see.

This included the wrongness in the pattern of my days. I was never meant to be stuffed away from light and air, nor hidden in a sprawling but spartan bachelor home, but these were the poles of my existence. I would be moved from pocket to wall and back again. In between, at times, I was brought into the open and looked at, sometimes turned about, sometimes lightly held. Then slid back down into darkness.

I had not always been alone. In my earliest time, I was surrounded by my exact matches. If you saw one of them, you saw me. When adjacent, we formed a perfect line ready to bind the fabric of the world.

Yes, that sounds grandiose, but it is true. We stood by as small servants for good, individually inglorious but collectively consequential. We mattered to our mistress, the finest of women, always diligent and industrious, continually contributing to the welfare of her struggling household. Her name was Belle.

Each of us was devoted to her. Under other circumstances, she would have dispatched us all at once. As it happened, she first chose only me. The others did stay together, and I was never missed. I know that, and, I know everything else. I'll tell it to you now.

When I enter the story, I will sometimes point myself out and sometimes not. Watch for me.

I

one

Mourning

Belle would have started work early in her life regardless, since her family needed her contribution, but it was all the earlier because her mother, Lily, died of consumption when Belle was still a girl. Archie and Lily had planned to have more children, but Belle was their only. After Lily's passing Archie never remarried. He continued toiling away at the humble craft of button-making.

In those days, buttons were a home industry. Archie was a master of shaping all of the materials involved: wood, bone, shell, animal horn. He molded pewter and stamped steel. All of this was to the specifications of dozens of local tailor and seamstress shops, including the covering of countless buttons in fabric chosen to complement garments. The cloth sheaths were the specialty of Lily, who could cut and sew tiny scraps with astonishing skill and speed. Fortunately, the work agreed with this duo. They seemed made for it, their contemplative minds receptive to repetition, their resilient frames comfortable with close work. What would have been tedious and wearing to others was satisfying and rewarding to them. They eked out a meager but content living.

But then Lily passed away.

Fortunately, Belle was able to pick up where her mother left off. In fact, it was a comfort to do so. It was what Lily had asked of Belle at the end, in thin breaths, between gulps for air.

"It's not looking good, Dearest. I shall hate to leave you. But it can't be helped. I'm glad you are here. To see me off. And to help your father. You have twice my skill. Twice my mind. Twice my heart. You are the bravest and best woman there ever was. I could not be more proud of you. And I will be proud of you in the next world. I will show you off. I will say, 'There is my Belle, helping her father. Loving her father. Look at her.' Look at you. Look at you. It's all I want to do. Look at you."

Heartbroken, tears streaming, Belle was at hand with Archie when Lily breathed her last.

At scarcely seven years of age, Belle had already worked beside her mother at every opportunity, and if anything, just as Lily proclaimed, she had even greater natural gifts. It always seemed to Archie that Belle could merely wave at materials and leave behind cloth-covered buttons. He mentioned this to Belle more than once after her mother died, and even Belle had to agree, because in a way, that's what happened. This was the miracle and mystery: Taking up the work daily ushered Belle into a blessed trance, transporting her to conversation with Lily. It was as if the movements—reaching for cloth, cutting it, threading needles, sewing—all of these constituted an incantation that counteracted and suspended time and death itself.

Belle would emerge from long communion with her mother only when the light started to fade, or when Archie would gently rock her shoulder to suggest that she cease. Belle would awaken from her reverie feeling that she had just taken her seat, only to find row upon precise row of perfectly-finished buttons. The only other sign of time's passing would be in her arms and hands: The glow and ache of all that she had done. And in her heart a glow and ache as well from impossibly seeing her mother again.

Her father had no such ability to reunite with his wife. Sadly, her death caused the usual separation. And so Archie and Belle carried on in their individual ways, turning out buttons and missing Lily. Each Sunday they visited her grave, with its tiny headstone and its slim neighboring empty plot for Archie, to chat with her. At parting, they left atop the headstone a button of a design that always differed from the time before. Each Sunday, the previous Sunday's tribute was absent, no doubt seized by someone even more needy than this bereft pair, in hopes of selling it or sewing it onto a patched and re-patched garment. Over ten years, Archie and Belle Endicott left five hundred and a score of buttons.

two

A visitor

Then one day, a visitor came to the Endicotts' humble shop and home. There were three crisp knocks. Wiping his hands on his smudged apron, Archie answered. The caller was a young man, long and lean with impressive side whiskers and a long navy coat. He took a step back from the door and removed his tall hat.

"Good day, sir. I am here to discuss a contract. My name is … "

He stopped as if he could not recall what he was called and peered over Archie's shoulder, his head cocked in curiosity. Archie turned to follow the gaze, and then he understood. The young man's eye had fallen on his daughter.

As was her gift, Belle's hands were floating and darting like butterflies as she used scissors, needle and thread to spirit fabric around buttons even as she gazed straight ahead with a soft smile and listened, it seemed, to someone beloved who was not there. Which, of course, was exactly what she was doing. She was with Lily.

A twinkle in his eye, Archie put a finger to his lips and beckoned the young man to enter. Sidewhiskers did so, his eyes never leaving Belle. In whispers, Archie explained Belle's unique state and skill. It warmed his heart to see Sidewhiskers' eyes narrow and his mouth flex in fascination.

"Extraordinary," Sidewhiskers murmured. "What an asset."

"Asset?" True to his name, Archie arched an eyebrow at this.

"A valuable capability, I mean."

"Oh, yes, she's a treasure, Belle is."

"Belle," said the young man softly.

"It means 'Beautiful' in French. Her mother spoke a bit of French."

"Indeed," said the young man. "Beautiful."

Archie could not be sure whether the visitor meant the girl or her "capability"—perhaps both—but he discovered an instant affection for him. Sidewhiskers was disarmingly awkward and nakedly ambitious. He had led with mention of a contract, and it appeared that he found Archie's and Belle's little family operation, to borrow the young man's phrase, valuable. How intriguing. Perhaps there was something good—and someone good?—here for Belle.

"You were about to say your name, sir?" said Archie.

"Indeed," said the young man, tearing his eyes from the girl and squaring again on her father. "My name is Ebenezer Scrooge."

three

Salutations

"I'm pleased to meet you, Mr. Scrooge. I am Archie Endicott."

Ebenezer shook Archie's hand briskly. "So I have been told. I was directed to you as the most knowledgeable of button-makers."

"Kind of people to say, sir."

"And that is who I seek—the finest button-maker. You see, I am entering the trade myself."

Archie's eyebrow arched again. "Indeed?" His amused affection also notched upward. This young man was offhandedly announcing himself a competitor.

"May I be frank, Mr. Endicott?"

"Archie, please."

The young man frowned. "May I not call you Mr. Endicott? I mean it with respect."

"You may not, sir," Archie said in a mock growl. "I do not object to your respect, which I will endeavor to earn, but if we are to be competitors, I want to also be friends, and friends use first names." He extended his hand again. "Agreed ... Ebenezer?"

Ebenezer was thrown into a pause. This was not going as he had expected. Mr. Endicott—er, Archie—was disturbingly cheerful. He reminded Ebenezer of his recent employer and mentor Fezziwig, God bless him. But at once he chided himself for drawing any comparison between a prosperous businessman and this proprietor of, literally, a cottage business. *The least of cottages, in fact,* thought Ebenezer, spurred by the meaning of the name "Endicott"—"the cottage on the end."

Still, any thought of Fezziwig brought a bloom of warmth to Ebenezer's chest. He steeled himself against welling up with emotion—Heaven forbid in front of a stranger—and sought to prevent any quaver in his voice with a vigorous reach for his host's hand.

"Agreed ... Archie," he said, holding the button-maker's brilliant blue eyes.

"Splendid!" Archie put his other hand atop Ebenezer's. "Now, my friend, let me pour tea while you tell me how you will run me out of business."

"Your words, not mine."

"You won't ruin me?" Archie's cheer belied his words as he bustled with the makings.

"I'm actually here about a sort of ... partnership."

"A partnership!" Archie said. "That does sound better than our losing everything. Do tell me what you have in mind."

four

Inside the factories

And so Ebenezer did. He explained that he meant to enter the button-making business from end opposite Archie's: High-volume manufacturing.

"I have seen the newest factories," Ebenezer said, "churning out buttons of steel, wood, bone, horn, mother-of-pearl, even gilt and silvered."

He described them in detail: Vast spaces thick with workers, many of them women and children, engaged in the various stages of production—punching, drilling, stamping, counter-sinking, staining, burnishing and more. Presses dropped buttons into troughs like rain. The largest of these machines were sunk into the ground beneath the floor for stability during the violent downward rammings. Side rooms lined with shelves stored vast arrays of metal dies, many of them retired shockingly quickly as fashions changed.

"How many dies might a factory have?" asked Archie.

"Oh, thousands."

"Thousands?" There was shock in Archie's voice.

"One factory might order a thousand new dies in one year. And retire hundreds of them."

"Each one stamping out buttons on machines?"

"By the thousand every hour."

Archie turned to his own molds and stamps, collected and crafted over decades, numbering in the dozens—the low dozens. What spun through his mind was how very many die-makers the factories must occupy. Each one making dies for machines that would continuously spit out buttons. Perhaps new dies were being made and discarded as quickly as Archie was making single buttons. He leaned back in his chair and took his time to produce one word: "Well."

Ebenezer waited, and Archie finally continued with a bemused smile.

"I feel sorry for you, Ebenezer."

"Sorry for me, Mist— Archie?"

"Of course! You have seen the wonders of the button factories and yet you come here to propose a partnership? You must have very poor judgment, lad."

The comment rendered Ebenezer speechless. Archie roared with laughter, and Ebenezer found himself doubled over as well.

five

First meeting

Their ruckus was enough to rouse Belle, who had remained busily sewing and communing with the spirit of Lily. Seeing his daughter's motions falter, Archie swiftly assumed his accustomed spot directly in front of her. He always took up this same position to serve as a consistent welcome when Belle ended her fantastic voyage. Ebenezer started to rise as well, but he froze when Archie waved behind his back for him to remain seated.

Belle returned to herself as was typical—with brief but pleasant confusion. She smiled at Archie, registered surprise at her own productivity, and stretched and rubbed her limbs while remaining seated. For the moment, Archie shielded Ebenezer from view.

"Hello, Father."

"Hello, Dearest. How is Mother?"

"She sends her love."

This exchange never varied, so this reunion was the same as ever—except for an indefinable something about Archie's posture that disclosed the presence of company. Belle tilted in her chair and peered around her father.

"Oh!" she said. She and Ebenezer rose together as if in a planned movement.

"Yes, Love, we have a guest, said Archie, also rising. "This is our new friend, Mr. Ebenezer Scrooge. Ebenezer, this is my darling Belle."

"How nice to meet you, Mr. Scrooge."

He took her small hand. "Ebenezer, please."

At Belle's hesitation, Archie piped up. "Yes, we're all on a first-name basis."

"Oh, already? Ebenezer then," Belle said.

"Belle," Ebenezer said. His soft, admiring utterance could have been mistaken for his speaking French.

"Please forgive me for not greeting you immediately," said Belle. "I was ... "

"... off visiting?" Ebenezer lightly slipped the suggestion into her pause.

"Just so," said Belle, smiling with mild surprise and looking at Archie.

"I explained," he said.

"I see."

"I'm glad for your ... unique opportunity," said Ebenezer.

His sincerity warmed Belle. As forbidding as was his first impression—tall, angular, dark hair, young brow already creased—she immediately felt at ease with this distinctively-named young man.

"Speaking of opportunity," said Archie. "Ebenezer sees one in our little shop."

"Here?" said Belle.

"Quite so," said Ebenezer. At last it was time to

explain why he had come. His answer condensed the account that follows.

six

A self-education

If traced all the way back, Ebenezer's visit to the Endicotts stemmed from his being a practical scholar.

As a boy, reading had been one of his few pleasures, aside from spending time with his younger sister Fan. Books let him escape a multitude of miseries—his frequently cruel father, his loneliness as an awkward boarding student, and the unrelenting grind of poverty. His first loves were fantastic adventure yarns—*One Thousand and One Nights*, *Valentine and Orson*, *Aladdin*, *Robinson Crusoe*. These tales carried him from his dismal surroundings just as Belle's reveries transported her from her loving but motherless home.

Ebenezer also found solace in his textbooks. They gave him topics and practices to understand and master. From his earliest school days he saw his books as a means to transform and even exalt himself, intuiting that the contents captured what accomplished persons would convey if he were able to compel them to teach him everything that they knew. The thought thrilled him. Was he not a king or a sorcerer, as from one of his story books, with power to summon throngs of authors? He could instantly dismiss any bores or fakers and as quickly call forth another writer in higher hopes.

That is, he could if another book was at hand. This was not always so during his leanest days, but he was never long without fresh reading material. His hunger for advancement was too great. He hunted books as a wolf stalks prey.

The young and ravenous Ebenezer was not above swiping books from passers-by or from shelves in the market. He deemed this a necessity of survival and ordained it a type of borrowing, since whenever possible he returned these volumes. More than once he reversed his pickpocketing and enjoyed imagining the book's owner discovering its magical reappearance.

Reading helped him grasp the notion of a career rather than a mere succession of jobs, and he studied various occupations. He began to actively seek particular commercial situations. His earliest apprenticeships taught him to consider more than the business itself, more than the employer, more than the wages. They taught him to seek opportunity to continue to read and educate himself. That was what brought him to Fezziwig.

seven

An interview

Ebenezer was on his third apprenticeship when he heard about an opening with Fezziwig and acquainted himself with the warehouse master's reputation. It was most attractive, but he forced himself not to be obsequious during his inquiry. He regarded himself as interviewing the prosperous old gentleman as much as the reverse. Something in Fezziwig's smile told him that this approach was welcome. Ebenezer coolly asked his crucial question: "Where do you stand on your apprentices reading?"

"Reading!" cried Fezziwigg. "The more the better! Not on the job, mind you, but off hours, the more time an apprentice gives himself to reading, the better I like it!"

Ebenezer's heart leapt, but he steeled himself to remain calm. "Do you provide books to apprentices?"

"Provide books?" Fezziwig's tone was inscrutable. Did the question seem impertinent? He rose and increased his volume. "Provide books to apprentices?"

Ebenezer looked him in the eye. "Do you, sir?"

"Come with me, young man." Fezziwig beckoned Ebenezer. They passed into an office and out its back, entering a large space with high windows.

"Behold!" said Fezziwig.

Ebenezer's mouth fell open. Books filled shelves from floor to ceiling. He quickly turned his head as if to peer elsewhere, but it was in fear that he might weep.

Giving no sign of noticing, Fezziwig was already on to the next room, again beckoning. He turned completely about and spread his hands in a flourish. "And behold!" he cried.

Hardly able to tear himself from the first room, Ebenezer stepped into an even larger collection. Four more walls of books.

By now, the boy's head was swimming. He tottered to a chair and openly stared.

"All yours to enjoy, Ebenezer," said Fezziwig, "if you'll work for me."

If! If! What a ridiculous word.

"When," said Ebenezer, "may I start?"

"Aha!" cried Fezziwig, extending his hand. "So happy to have you!"

Ebenezer rose for the handshake and found himself dazedly grinning. He preferred to carry a serious expression, but just then he could not help but beam.

"You may start immediately," Fezziwig said.

"Thank you, sir. Just let me stow my coat, and I'll get right to it."

"Oh, not work, my boy! Tomorrow is soon enough for that. I meant that you may immediately begin to read!"

Another giddy wave washed over Ebenezer, but he managed to reply soberly, "Most kind of you, sir."

"I can see the hunger in your eyes, I can," said Fezziwig. "Choose any books you like. Take 'em home, and bring them back for more!"

eight

Enjoyable work

And so it began—a glorious decade with Fezziwig. Marvelous, metamorphic years packed with work, books, mishaps and lessons. There was the time that Ebenezer had to chase a team of horses spooked by mice that suddenly streamed from a load of grain. There was the time that his thumb was mashed between a tipping crate and a pillar, and blood poured under his nail until it had to be pierced with a hot needle to relieve the pressure. There was the time that he and fellow apprentice Dick Wilkins surprised Fezziwig by staying through the night to complete paperwork for a huge shipment whose arrival date moved up. Fezziwig had nearly shaken off their hands in giving thanks. He even sent out to a tavern for breakfast, and he and Mrs. Fezziwig themselves served Dick and Ebenezer.

And the parties! Ebenezer had to admit that he

enjoyed them. At holidays and at random times of the Fezziwigs' choosing, he and Dick transformed the mammoth warehouse into the brightest and coziest of spaces. Ebenezer mainly kept to himself at these affairs, content to watch and know that his efforts had made all of it possible. He would lean back and impassively survey the frivolity, imagining the revelers indebted to him. It only enhanced his pleasure to know that no such thought would occur to any of the attendees. He was one strain of being, they another.

nine

The day approaches

Kindly allow, Dear Reader, a swerve to the past of Belle Endicott, where you will find distinct differences from and striking similarities to the story of Ebenezer Scrooge.

It was exactly one week short of one year after Lily's passing that Belle first saw her again. After negotiating each season without her mother, she and Archie were now well acquainted with her absence. The world no longer seemed utterly void. They still wore the blacks and grays of mourning but had progressed to lighter shades and discussed when to return to garments with color.

"I have dreamed of seeing my Blue Bell again," Archie said.

"And you have seen my rainbow, Father." Belle meant the abutted curves of buttons, an orderly arrangement of all hues, that adorned the shabby shelf in her room.

"I have. You honor me."

"It gave me an idea."

"Oh?"

"But it's a surprise."

"Ah, so I'll just have to wait."

"Yes, until the thirteenth."

"Of next month?"

"Yes."

This would be the first anniversary of Lily's passing.

"The thirteenth sounds like the perfect day for a rainbow surprise."

"Or maybe the fourteenth?"

"Well, it's up to you. Why would you want the thirteenth, or why the fourteenth?"

"The thirteenth, because that was … that was the day. And this surprise would make her happy. The fourteenth because … no, not the fourteenth. That would mean that the thirteenth can only be sad."

"Keep it sad, you mean."

"Yes, and she wouldn't want any of her days reserved for sadness."

"I must agree. The thirteenth then."

"I can't wait!"

Belle fell to her button-cover sewing filled with warmth, as if she had touched her mother's mind. In and out her needle went. In out in out in out in out, then …

In a chair opposite her sat Lily. She had sewing of her own, and the movements of her needle mirrored Belle's.

ten

Impossible reunion

Look at you, Belle Endicott.

Mother.

Baby Girl.

Mother.

Baby Girl, all grown up.

Mother. How—?

How is the question about everything, isn't it, Dear? How did I get a husband as grand as Archie? How did we get a girl as marvelous as you?

But how … ?

I don't know, child. But now we get this.

But—

Let's try this—let's just talk. Because that is what we always did in the shop working. And that's where we are.

We are in the shop.

Tell me whatever you like.

I— You— You can't believe how I've missed you, Mother. It burns like fire.

I know, Dearest. I know the agony.

Why did you— But no, I can't ask you that …

You can ask me anything, my sweet.

Why did you leave me? Leave us? No, no, I'm sorry, I'm sorry, I—

No, Belle, it's all right. It's not wrong to ask.

Then … why?

I could not help it. My body withered.

I know, I know. I just—

You are angry at me.

Oh, no, no, Mother, I—

You are, sweetheart, and it's all right. I know that I always seemed to have my way—directing your father this way and that, able to enforce what I wanted. But that was in the every-

day. The eternal—my own life—was not in my control.

I know, Mother, I do know. I just— It's what my heart asks. From pain. Does that make sense?

Yes, of course it does. The heart asks what it wants to ask and needs to ask. It doesn't have sense. The mind has sense. Let the heart speak, always. The mind will speak in its own time.

Ah, Mother. I feel better now.

Not angry?

No, it's gone.

Good.

Thank you, Mother.

Of course, Darling. Now what else will you tell me?

I— I— I can't think of anything. You made my mind stop!

Well, what about your surprise?

My surprise?

The one for the thirteenth, the idea that came from your rainbow of buttons.

Oh, yes, that! This is exciting! I'm going to—

But next time, Dearest. Tell me next time.

No, Mother. Don't go! Wait!

I'm sorry, Dear Belle. I have to, for now.

No! Not again!

It's only for a short time.

Mother!

You'll see me next time you sew. I promise.

Lily swirled away, dissolving from the world again, and all of the torment flooded back inside Belle. She writhed at it, then felt the touch of gentle hands.

"Belle, sweetheart. Belle."

She opened her eyes to Archie.

"Are you all right?" Archie said. "I was calling, and you didn't answer."

Her face filled with confusion.

"Belle, honey, what— ?"

A year of pain sucked away from her, replaced by bliss. Belle surged at her father with a joyful shriek.

eleven

A concern

The following week set the pattern for the next ten years. Belle immediately stopped needing to know how it was possible to visit the deceased. She and Archie were simply astonished and grateful.

Belle sewed her way back to Lily each day, under Archie's dumbfounded (and initially envious) gaze. They soon established their routine for her departures and returns.

"Hello, Father."

"Hello, Dearest. How is Mother?"

"She sends her love."

After a few days, Belle explained to Archie that she needed one evening in her room alone with Lily, to work on her surprise for him. They agreed that if Archie feared she was lingering too long, he would knock on the door to rouse her, but then wait for her answer, to give her time to hide her work.

Though Archie assured Belle that she never spoke during her reveries, this arrangement also gave her ease about asking Lily a question that was plaguing her.

Why can't Father see you?

I don't know that any more than I know why you can see me.

Perhaps because he doesn't sew?

Oh, he sews. He's a master! You inherited as much or more of your sewing skill from him as from me. Don't you and he ever talk? Hasn't he told you he was a tailor?

Father was a tailor?

An excellent tailor.

But that can't be!

Why not?

Well, he's so shy! When Father and I take the buttons to the shops, the tailors always have customers there, measuring them and listening to what they want. How could Father ever have talked that much?

That's exactly why your papa is no longer a tailor. He is kind and patient, of course, but he likes to keep to himself. Or to our little family. The rest of the world quickly makes him weary.

So he switched to buttons. Ah! I like that for him.

Yes, it's been perfect. He was already tied to the right people: tailors know other tailors and seamstresses, and they all need buttons. Your father saw that he could switch to making buttons and avoid meeting all the people directly. It was work that I enjoyed as well.

Maybe he did tell me this.

I'm sure that he did.

I don't always pay attention.

I know, and we have to talk about that.

What do you mean?

I'm not satisfied with your education, Belle. It's not training your mind well enough.

What do you mean, Mother?

The part-time school is not challenging you. It needs to be harder.

Harder? But isn't— ? Hmpf.

I know what you're thinking: Isn't everything hard enough? Just getting to school and putting up with this boy and that girl, though many are very nice, and sitting through the lessons and working all the time when you're home …

Can you read my thoughts, Mother?

As much as any mother can read her child's thoughts, yes. Maybe just a little more.

Well, I do think everything you just said. Things are hard enough, and you want to make them harder? It's—

Say it, Belle. It's all right.

It's hard enough having a ghost mother who I don't even know is really there!

I know, Dear.

It's what my heart thinks, so I had to say it.

I'm glad you did.

And now you want to make my school harder?

Yes.

Hmpf.

It's because I can see the woman you will become. Not because I died and know the future. I don't. I would be able to see this if I were still with you every day. When you grow up and see yourself and others change, you can see the steps in between, and you can see something of how the future will unfold. You are a strong, wise, smart girl, and you will only grow more so, but only if you are nurtured, like a plant. Remember when we went out and saw the farm?

Oh, yes, the calf!

Yes, the calf. And the corn, which had to be tended with water and fertilizer. The farmer had to pull weeds and keep away birds. You are your own plant. For you, pulling weeds and keeping away birds is keeping yourself from dirty, lazy minds who would do you harm. Your water and fertilizer is your family, your church, your school and especially reading on your own.

Reading? I love it!

I know you do.

But books are hard to find.

Not if you know where to look.

Where should I look?

twelve

A promise

It will take effort. You'll need to work at borrowing books from everyone you know—members of the church and teachers. Tailors and seamstresses and their customers who would be kind enough to lend to you. Let it be known in the shops that you want to borrow any and all kinds of books and that you always return them on time, clean and intact. I want you to read one book per week.

A book every week?

Yes. Books are teachers and friends. Through them you can learn anything and go anywhere. Our little shop is a world unto itself, but it is within a giant world and a larger universe. Please promise me you will do this. I learned to treasure books late in my short life, through our friend at church, Mrs. Burt. You know her.

Oh, yes! Her pure white hair. She already lets Father and me borrow books. We're very careful to take them back every Sunday.

Yes, I felt sure she would. She loaned me books, and we talked about them after worship. She opened my eyes about books providing education. This is the best thing you will ever do for yourself, for your father and for me. A book a week. Promise me, Belle?

I promise, Mother. A book a week.

Good girl.

A book a week! Belle was taken with the idea, all the more because it was at the behest of Lily. She saw the opportunity to please her, and it would always give them things to talk about.

Within five years, Belle was reading two books a week. By then, little cards with her name and address were well known in all the tailor and seamstress shops, as well as in local pubs and taverns:

BOOKS WANTED
I borrow and return books clean and intact.
Please inquire at Endicott Button.

Over the years, she and Lily discussed countless corners of existence. Belle recorded the title and author of every book that she read, as well as her thoughts on it. After filling many journals, she decided to create a ledger of the topics that she seemed to return to, and she brought this up to date at the close of every year, resolving to read at least one book in each area in the ensuing twelve months. When Ebenezer Scrooge appeared at the shop, Belle's alphabetized topics list was as follows:

Animals, especially birds, cats and dogs.
Art of all kinds: drawing, painting, music, sculpture, theater.
Business and work.
Capabilities, especially learning, memory and perception.
Emotion, especially love, motivation and satisfaction.
Food.
Government.
Health, especially disease, exercise and medicine.
Holidays.
Human behavior.
Language and communication.
Money.
Nature.
Reading, writing and books.
Recreation including athletics and games.
Relationships of all types: family, friendship, partnership, romance.
Religion and philosophy.
Sleep and dreams.
Technology.

Time.
Transportation.
Travel and all foreign lands.
Weather.

Thus did Belle Endicott become one of the few young citizens of London as well read as Ebenezer Scrooge.

Oh, Reader! Let us skip back to the first anniversary of Lily's passing, on the thirteenth of the month. Belle proudly presented Archie with a garment that he already owned, newly adorned with fasteners that he himself had made: His favorite soft gray cardigan was now resplendent with buttons in the colors of the rainbow from top to bottom: red, orange, yellow, green, blue and violet. A chilly evening at home never passed without his donning this sweater. On the other side of the fire would be Belle with a book.

thirteen

A departure

Back to young Mr. Scrooge.

Eventually, everything good about his time with Fezziwig was not good enough for Ebenezer to stay on. The plan that he developed even led him to shun a proposal from Fezziwig to become his partner and eventually own the business. Ebenezer had not announced his intention to leave, but Fezziwig had somehow divined his thoughts. He asked Ebenezer for a private word and made his generous offer.

Ebenezer gave an appearance of considering it but then said, "As thankful as I am to have been in your employ, sir, and as honored as I am by what you propose, I must decline."

"Will you tell me why?" said Fezziwig.

Ebenezer's grandly-embroidered reply was: "My decision comes from my conviction that I cannot fully grasp all that I have learned throughout my career, and particularly what I have gleaned from you, if I do not establish an enterprise where none existed previously. I want to contend with every stage of commercial development, so as to appreciate the full nature of the institution."

"You want to start from nothing and know everything," rephrased Fezziwig cordially.

Ebenezer inclined toward him in a sort of full-body nod.

"Know everything about building a firm, yes."

"Everything," reiterated Fezziwig jovially.

Ebenezer vaguely realized that Fezziwig knew that he ultimately wanted to trust only his own judgment in all things and felt that this would be to his protege's detriment. Ebenezer disagreed. Fezziwig made a point of gathering opinions from any and all before making business decisions—from brother to banker to boy on the corner—and this nearly drove Ebenezer mad.

As if wisdom were scattered equally amongst all people, he scoffed to himself, *rather than concentrated in the more industrious and perspicacious, such as authors and persons of business. What a waste of time is random consultation.*

Ebenezer was determined to continually absorb information so as to become his own walking library. He methodically organized his self-education in all areas of commerce, carrying a small notebook to capture topics that he wanted to master. He filled and retired dozens of these journals and drew great satisfaction from storing them neatly, a testament to his burgeoning mastery. Gaining knowledge was a way to become a world unto oneself, reliant on no one. During times of calamity, there had to be those to whom others would turn.

Some need to look to others, but not I, thought Ebenezer. *I was made to be the one looked to.*

This revelation made sense of his childhood. His punishing, penurious youth taught him early in life that he could rely only on himself. What a head start that was.

Now came the next stage of his destiny. He gave notice to Fezziwig, who reluctantly received it. He was humbled by Fezziwig's generous parting bonus and warm wishes. He left later that month with his eye on the button trade.

fourteen

A new industry

Mechanization was on the rise, and Ebenezer had visited several button-making factories. This was because Fezziwig's great friend Jeremy Tiffle, a tailor, had been approached by the earliest of the modernizing button suppliers, and he introduced Fezziwig to several firms who became his warehouse customers. Fezziwig asked for tours of the factories and was able to include Ebenezer, who quickly became enamored of the industry. He favored buttons as items for warehousing because the individual containers were relatively easy to handle and store, particularly in contrast to the ponderous bolts of cloth that Fezziwig warehoused and had to carefully guard from dust and moisture. Garment-making supplies were a specialty of the Fezziwig operation.

Ebenezer also liked the button factories in their own right, finding much to fascinate him. Many buttons were akin to elaborate medallions—indeed the factories often produced medals as well—and the crafting of the dies was exacting in both their designs—precise, miniature likenesses of people, places, objects and animals—and in the delicate production process, which sometimes resulted in multiple castings due to cracks at the very last stage. Ebenezer had a remarkable capacity for detail and systematic approaches, and he was sure that he would do well in this industry.

Grandly-engraved buttons appealed to him in another way. This art would place him amongst the finest of things, which is where he was convinced he belonged. He had come to straightforwardly recognize his gifts. What sense did it make to pooh-pooh his own admirable capabilities?

He was also attracted to the many transitions involved in the button industry, centering around the continual introduction of new styles of fashion. One of the countless books that he consumed had expounded that a thriving enterprise will, in essence, put itself out of business by becoming the company that would otherwise do so, depriving another organization of the opportunity to triumph. Ebenezer liked the idea of hastening and even inviting change.

One final note on what appealed to Ebenezer about button-making: The various materials brought connections to far-flung lands. There were pearls from Tahiti and Hawaii, shells from the Gulf of Mexico, Manila or Singapore, wood from spots as distant as Brazil and Madagascar. Each button was a tiny portal to the world.

This broad interest in, excitement about, and

affection for button manufacturing was the backdrop of Ebenezer's visit to the humble Endicott home. He had studied the most minute of production details, and he was determined to optimize every link in the chain and develop the finest top-to-bottom operation in all the world. He would rule nothing less than an empire.

fifteen

A proposal

"Well," said Archie and Belle simultaneously after Ebenezer conveyed the preceding, albeit in much shorter and less revealing fashion.

"Indeed," said Ebenezer.

"And yet you insist you have not come simply to announce that our end is nigh?" said Archie.

Belle looked at him quizzically.

"Before you joined us, Dear, I suggested this to Ebenezer, and he demurred."

Belle turned to Ebenezer. "It does sound rather hopeless for us, friend."

"Quite the opposite, I assure you."

"Then you have come to give us hope?"

"I bring you hope in this form." Ebenezer drew a document from his jacket. "A contract for sewing. The aspect of button manufacturing that has thus far resisted mechanizing is the attachment of buttons to strips of cloth, which is often the preferred way to package and present them—but of course you know that already." He gestured to strips of buttons at hand. "I am prepared to offer you all the work you can handle in that regard—and then some. You would be in a position to hire help yourselves."

Archie and Belle once again reclined and looked at each other. Finally, Archie spoke.

"No more actual making of buttons, then? Exclusively sewing buttons onto cloth?"

"Yes and no," said Ebenezer. "Yes, you would discontinue your current method of production. Like it or not, manufacturing is the future of buttons. They will cease to be made by hand. If you had not heard this from me, you would soon have heard it from another."

"I have no doubt," sighed Archie. "I've seen this in bits and pieces from my own customers. Some of them have turned to other sources, and I can't say I blame them for choosing greater variety at lower cost. My business has already slowed." He removed his glasses and rubbed his eyes. "It's hard to let go of a lifetime's trade, and it's poor timing for you, Dearest." He said this last looking at Belle.

"Oh, Father."

"Or the perfect timing," said Ebenezer.

Belle raised an eyebrow at him.

"Because of my proposal," said Ebenezer, brandishing the contract. "The sewing work. And supervising other sewers." A thought occurred to him here. "May I ask— Or, no, it would be improper."

"Is it about my mother?"

"I'm afraid so. I— "

"No, no, it's perfectly fine. You wondered whether I would be able to commune with her if our work should change?"

"I did."

"Not to worry. If I take up a different type of sewing or other silent, methodical work, so will she, in her own way. It is kind of you to inquire." Ebenezer nodded in acknowledgment.

"And if I supervise other sewers, as I sometimes have done during pressing periods, that would still leave me plenty of work in solitude."

"If you take up a different kind of work, you say, Dearest," said Archie, stressing the word 'If.' "Do you see another choice?"

"In a world of button factories, Father, no, I do not. But we need to hear more from Ebenezer." She looked to him. "In particular, I wonder: Why us, specifically? To work for you?"

"Also," said Archie, "you said Yes and No about the work being only sewing of buttons onto cloth. What did you mean?"

"My answer to both questions is one word," said Ebenezer. "Expertise."

He punctuated this by rising. "You know buttons in your souls. I can see that in your work, and in the recommendations that I received from the tailor and seamstress shops. When I inquired about handmade buttons, your name, Mr. Endicott, rose to the top of the list." Here he produced a pocket journal and read notes of praise: "Utterly dependable ... Unfailingly conscientious ... Unmatched craftsmanship ... Pride in the work ... Pleasant and witty in the bargain ..."

"Pshaw." Archie waved away the compliments. "Though I don't mind hearing all that!" He winked at Belle and gestured to her. "Everything applies as much and more to my darling girl."

"Witty, Father? That remark was not for me."

"True, that one's for me alone." Archie's guffaw drew the same from Belle but this time only a smile from Ebenezer.

"In all seriousness," he said, raising his notebook. "I am here because of these superlatives. To be blunt, as we have discussed, many traditional button-makers will soon be out of business and seeking new work. It only makes sense for me to draw on this reservoir of ability as I fill my positions for sewing and other tasks. I do not only want to buy hands, I want to reward minds and to partner with those who savor detail as I do. I want every worker of mine to be the ideal person for that position. Between two sewers of buttons onto cloth, I prefer the one capable of more than the sewing, who sees the sewing within the larger whole. As much as possible, I want workers who look at the work as I do—nay, better than I ever could due to incomparable experience, but with the same desire to make the best items of their kind."

"Fervently said, sir!" said Archie.

"I wonder you don't go into parliament," said Belle.

"In due time," said Ebenezer, with dryness that echoed Archie's. "Business first, broader society later." It was not like him to joke in this way. The Endicotts' spirit had made him giddy.

sixteen

A farewell

A moment of stillness descended. Ebenezer had shared his wider and narrower goals, and they settled across the shop like birds coming to rest.

"It is hard to let go," Archie repeated with a sigh. Belle patted his hand as he addressed their guest.

"You are a thoughtful young man, Ebenezer Scrooge. It is kind of you to seek us out and share so much with us. Indeed, with our livelihood withering as we have discussed, you are acting as an agent of warning and providence, perhaps sent by an influence in the great beyond."

Her father's suggestion made Belle's face crumple with feeling. She drew a handkerchief from a pocket.

"Whatever happens to Belle and me," continued Archie, "I wish you the very best, young man. You have impressive zeal. So much that I fear for you."

"Fear for me, sir? —Archie?"

"A mite, yes. I see that you have good judgment after all, but ... Well, may the intensity of your own intention not sweep you away, friend." His bright blue eyes were trained on the young man. "You have high aims. It will take much to pursue them. I know this while possessed of far thinner powers than your own. Even maintaining this poor little shop"—he swept his hand about—"took everything that we three could muster. The most modest enterprise is a struggle that drains the soul. And you are on the threshold of forming a grand operation. There will be dark times, son. Do not let them turn you dark."

Ebenezer's throat stiffened. He recalled similar notes of caution from Fezziwig. Ebenezer could hear his old master now, addressing him in private, his normally-booming voice softened: "Be still at times, my boy, not always on the move. Take moments to reflect." And another urging: "You are not only what you do, Ebenezer. Activity makes a man neither better nor worse. It merely reveals what he values. Do not chase your worth or seek to establish it. You own it already."

Ebenezer flashed on a time when two young women had simultaneously spurned him just outside of Fezziwig's warehouse. As he and his employer exited, Ebenezer had tipped his hat as the ladies rolled past in an open-top carriage. In perfect unison, both riders swiveled their parasols so as to block him from view.

Fezziwig, who had been occupied locking the front

door, turned just in time to witness the encounter. With both hands, he flicked imagined dust from Ebenezer's shoulders, brushing off each of the supercilious maidens.

"Efficient elimination, my boy," he said. "Two with one tip of the hat."

Ebenezer recalled angling his chin at Fezziwig to indicate that, as far as he was concerned, there had been no maidens in no carriage.

With Archie, Ebenezer angled his chin and set his mouth in the same way.

"Kind words that I shall recall, Archie. Thank you."

"You are most welcome, lad. Thank you for your offer."

"I thank you as well, Ebenezer," said Belle, "for your proposal and for imparting the praise that my father so richly deserves. And for your interest in my odd visits to my mother."

"Please forgive my intruding at such a time."

She waved this aside. "It's best that you know, if we are to be business associates." Again, she put a light spin on the word "if."

"May I see the contract?" Archie said. He and Belle read it together.

Belle turned to Ebenezer. "May we have the evening to discuss this?"

"By all means. Shall I return at this same time tomorrow?"

"Please."

"I look forward to it."

"As do we," said Archie. He saw their visitor out with a firm handshake. Just before he turned away, Ebenezer's eye fell on Belle one last time over Archie's head.

Father and daughter briefly regarded each other in silence, then drew in breaths to repeat that same word: "Well."

"Let us speak of this after visiting your mother," suggested Archie.

"Oh, Father! I was thinking just the same."

As Ebenezer withdrew, he slipped something from the smaller pocket inside his jacket and regarded it with fresh eyes. It was a card that he had seen in virtually all of the tailor and seamstress shops where he had sought recommendations.

BOOKS WANTED
I borrow and return books clean and intact.
Please inquire at Endicott Button.

seventeen

A special visit

Before they left the shop, Belle carefully selected a button to leave on her mother's headstone. In keeping with established ritual, she veiled her choice from Archie to see only when Lily also did. Also as always, father and daughter held hands throughout their walk, separating when they arrived. Archie removed his hat.

"Hello, Old Girl," he addressed Lily.

"We brought you something, Mother," said Belle, setting the button in place.

Now Archie saw it. "Our finest work," he beamed.

"Only our best for you, Mum."

"The shop had a visitor today, Dearest," said Archie. "A young man."

"A most earnest young man," said Belle, playfully making her voice low and serious.

"Tall," said Archie.

"Serious," said Belle, adding more bass to her voice.

"Thoughtful."

"Most full of thoughts, Mother."

"And with a great interest in buttons."

"A burgeoning button baron."

"He gave us much to consider, Lil."

"Oh, not so much. Only the demise of all we have ever known."

"But also a partnership."

"A type of partnership."

"Perhaps this would put us in a coach climbing a mountain, upward to the peak."

"Or leave us foundered in a ditch."

"Which is where we appear to be headed without this young man, at any rate."

"So it might only be a matter of speed, Mother."

"Or a matter or survival."

"In short," said Belle, "we are doing well."

"And our options have grown," said Archie.

Belle nodded, her expression transforming. "Oh, I miss you, Mama," she breathed, tilting her head into her hands. Archie went to her side with his handkerchief. They traded it back and forth to dry their eyes.

Belle finally spoke again. "I do miss you, Mother, but I'm glad you are not here for these hard times. Change can be frightening."

Archie peered at her softly, and Belle found his eye.

"But one way or another, change is what we'll have," she said.

Soon they left, arm in arm and passed through the gate.

Across the way, a figure separated itself from the shadow on the far side of the caretaker building. It was a tall young man. He slowly approached Lily's headstone, glancing now and again after the departing pair, careful to remain unseen. He doffed his hat and held it before him solemnly as he took in the carving on the stone. Noticing what lay on top—the button—he found himself reaching for it.

When he slipped away, the button was in his pocket.

eighteen

Pocketed

I, Dear Reader, was in the pocket of Ebenezer Scrooge. A lowly but much esteemed button. There have I remained ever since. Not in the very same pocket, of course. Many different trousers and jackets over many decades. But always a pocket of Mr. Ebenezer Scrooge.

It is a wonder that I have not been lost. Actually, I have been lost, many times. Mr. Scrooge has misplaced me and proceeded to tear apart his surroundings in search of me, retracing his steps in his quarters or his office, or both, for hours or even days. On each occasion, to his trembling relief, he ultimately found me. Nay, I must correct myself: He did not always exhibit relief. Sometimes it was with volcanic anger that he finally spied me, one time snatching me and holding me in both of his hands and beginning to try to bend me so as to crack and ruin me. (It would not be an easy feat, I must say. Have you ever tried to break a button with your fingers?) But his rage abated, or at least paused, long enough that he changed his mind and merely flung me across the room. I ricocheted into a deucedly obscure crevice that cost Mr. Scrooge another week of searching. When he found me again, he briefly wept. Then with grave concentration he threaded a black cord through one of my eyes, transforming me into something of a necklace never to adorn a neck. Or think of me as a one-button string for prayer that Mr. Scrooge religiously hung beside his bed every night before sleeping.

Religion? Prayer? Did Mr. Scrooge pray? I will say this: He pondered. He brooded. He mused. And he always reached for me at such times. He idly swung me on the cord or wrapped it around his fingers and held me lightly as he sat back in his chair and looked at nothing. Or found me in his pocket as he took long walks through the streets of London, often under the veil of night. The very definition of standoffish, Mr. Scrooge continually kept company only with his thoughts.

I know what ran through his mind: His failure.

Are you shocked? The mighty Ebenezer Scrooge, who came to represent the height of material success, whose fortune grew even larger than rumored, who openly disdained those whose accomplishments were pale imitations of his own ... preoccupied with failure? Surely I jest!

I do not. He could never release the times when he fell short. He always muttered about it to himself in the singular—"Do you forget your failure?"—appending this to address whatever arena was rankling him at the moment:

"Do you forget your failure in business?"

"Do you forget your failure to represent your own interests?"

"Do you forget your failure to keep your promise to yourself?"

Each particular failure was the totality of his defeats. Whatever worked in his endeavors was offset by what had not succeeded. It was self-flagellation in the extreme. This went on for all of the decades that I spent with him.

I did witness failure. His button factory was pushed to the brink when—

But wait, that links to the decision that Archie and Belle made regarding Ebenezer's proposal, so let us fly back to their next meeting with him, when he arrived in Archie's shop. Little did the Endicotts know that I was returning to my birthplace, as it were, in the company of my new owner.

nineteen

A counter-proposal

"So pleased to see you again, Ebenezer," said Archie. Belle inclined her head in assent.

"I am pleased to return, and hopeful that you will join my business."

"As to that," said Archie. "We have a counter-proposal."

"Oh?" said Ebenezer. His bearing stiffened.

"We appreciate your offer of employment, but your contract specifies an exclusive relationship, to begin immediately."

"Yes, of course. Immediately because I am eager to profit from my investments. And exclusivity is a common business practice, to ensure reliable supply and deprive competitors of the same source."

"For the present, Ebenezer," said Belle, "we must remain one of those competitors, paltry as our efforts might be."

Scrooge released a breath as if he had been struck.

"We have no doubt," continued Archie, "that our current business will shrivel as manufactured buttons gain sway. But the change will take time. And the customers who rely on us today—we cannot leave them tomorrow. We have orders to fill."

Scrooge struggled for composure. "I understand your sense of loyalty, and of course, your commitment to your contracts. I would have it no other way. When will they be satisfied? Will you accept my proposal then?"

"The orders will not take long to fill," Archie said. "Two weeks at most. We have never run far ahead in our business. It has always been hand-to-mouth."

"Will you join my business in two weeks, then?"

"We don't know yet," said Belle. "We have to speak to the holder of each account, to seek his or her preference. If a given shop wants to place more orders, we will also honor those."

"That could continue indefinitely," noted Ebenezer.

"It could," said Belle. "But we consider it only proper. These customers have sustained us for decades."

"In the meantime," said Archie, "I cannot sign your agreement."

Ebenezer fell as still as a statue, looking at the floor, deliberating. Finally he turned to Archie. "You mentioned a counter-proposal?"

"Something for your consideration," said Archie. He looked to Belle to proceed.

"It has to do with fashion," she said. "Which is often a matter of uniqueness, of course. Not wanting to wear what everyone else is wearing. There is always a demand for a distinct design or color or fabric ... and even distinct fasteners. While large-scale manufacturing, of course, aims for just the opposite: Producing a lot of the same. So that, for example, any number of garments have the same buttons."

"At a much lower cost per piece," said Ebenezer.

"No doubt," said Archie. "And that will be of great benefit to most, cutting the cost of clothing."

"But for some cost is not the primary concern," said Belle. "While uniqueness is. There are those who are willing to pay more to remain distinct, even down to the fasteners on their garments. The fewer made of a given button, the better."

"And if there is any way that our little shop can outdo a factory," Archie said lightly, "it is in producing fewer buttons."

"Unique buttons," said Belle. "Handmade in what will soon be the old-fashioned way."

"But you are pitting the weakness of the past against the strength of the future," Ebenezer protested. "It is sending— " He groped for an analogy. "It is dispatching an ailing David against a robust Goliath. How can you hope to survive? And not simply be swept aside?"

"That is not what we see," said Belle. "What we see is different strengths and an alternative story: Let us say David and Goliath— " She, too, grasped for an illustration. " —both working for Abraham."

"But Abraham lived long before David and— "

"Pardon me for interrupting, Ebenezer, but you miss my point. Imagine David and Goliath removed from war and placed in the commercial enterprises of Abraham, who needed intrepid shepherds as well as hulking bodyguards—both David and Goliath. Neither could do what the other could, but Abraham needed each, and his efforts prospered."

"Abraham did prosper," said Ebenezer. "He became the wealthiest man in the world, with the services of neither David nor— "

"But he would have had the equivalent, don't you see? His own Davids and Goliaths providing a range of specific abilities. Abraham engaged all of them."

"In your analogy, then, Abraham is ... ?"

"Abraham is the range of need in the marketplace. Certainly, most shops will come to prefer manufactured buttons. But not all. Some tailors will want to offer exclusive buttons."

"This is your conjecture."

"True," said Belle, "It is speculation. But it is based on our sense of things."

"When we spoke yesterday," said Archie, "you placed value on our insight."

"Yes, indeed, but what I meant was ... What I expected was ..."

Archie's eyebrows rose.

"Suggestions that match your own understanding?" offered Belle. "And do not challenge it?"

Ebenezer dropped the bridge of his nose between two fingers. This conversation, and in some small but important way, his entire nascent effort, seemed to be getting away from him.

twenty

Slow understanding

"I do want your ideas," Ebenezer said. "I am straining to comprehend. Let us say that you are correct—that, at times, in particular situations, some tailor and seamstress shops will want to purchase buttons as they did in the past."

"Exactly," said Belle.

"Old-fashioned buttons," reiterated Archie.

"Nostalgic buttons," said Ebenezer.

"You say it with derision, sir," said Belle.

"Forgive me, please. I am still struggling to understand."

"Are you? Or are you determined to find fault or weakness?"

"When I receive a suggestion, shall I not challenge it?"

Belle recognized the echo of her earlier words. "Well put," she said. "Let us continue in good faith."

"Let us allow," said Ebenezer in the same spirit, "a demand for old-fashioned buttons."

"Nostalgic," said Archie.

"Yes," said Ebenezer. "But how great is the demand? And from which shops will it come?"

"That, Ebenezer," said Belle, "is where Father and I do see the benefit of becoming partners. We assume that you will have a person visiting shops to introduce your lines of buttons, yes?"

"Three representatives, actually."

"Three," said Archie, impressed.

"Paid on commission, with generous incentives to write orders." He corrected himself. "Actually, to begin with, six representatives."

"Six!" Archie and Belle said.

"Reduced to five after the first week, four after the second, and three after the third," said Ebenezer. "Leaving the three most productive."

Belle took this in. "A struggle to survive."

"In which each of us engages, whether or not we consider it," said Ebenezer. "I want to identify those representatives most attuned to the competitive situation and suited to engage in it heartily."

"Your representatives know of this arrangement?" said Archie.

"They will after the first week," said Ebenezer.

"Bold of you, sir," said Belle.

"As bold as David offering Goliath a counter-proposal," Ebenezer said with a slight bow.

"Which is this," Belle said, her eyes dancing. "Your swiftly-winnowed representatives will visit many tailor and seamstress shops, I am sure—"

"Each one in London," interjected Ebenezer. "And beyond."

"Ambitious!" said Archie.

"—and Father and I speculate," Belle continued jauntily, "that they might find it useful to be able to offer our 'Nostalgic Buttons,' if you will, when they seem to better suit the proprietor's interests."

"A secondary line of products," murmured Ebenezer.

"Precisely," said Belle.

She saw that their prospective partner had finally caught the vision. Everything about him quickened. "A secondary line," he repeated.

"Precisely!" said Archie, winking at Belle.

"A small shop within your large shop," said Belle, "promoted by your representatives."

"Salesmen, I call them."

"Ah, yes! A good term."

Their shining eyes locked on each other.

"Brilliant," said Ebenezer. "Now I understand, and I agree."

"Very well!" said Archie.

"Very well," said Ebenezer, now fully taken with the idea, gazing off and repeating, "A secondary line of products."

Archie and Belle smiled at each other and mouthed the words as Ebenezer said them again: "Very well."

II

twenty-one

Sharing the news

Things did go well.

Archie and Belle signed Ebenezer's agreement and immediately began to supplement his representatives, visiting each of their customers and explaining their new relationship with a button manufacturer. They met a range of reactions. Some customers were aghast and immediately placed large orders so as to ensure future supplies.

One elderly and erudite tailor, Charles Gabriel, was thoroughly scandalized.

"How can you even consider cooperating with an enterprise such as you describe?" he scolded. "It is utterly devoid of human spirit, reducing workers to unthinking pieces of machinery. How degrading."

Belle blinked but managed to reply warmly. "Your heart for your fellow man has always been evident, Mr. Gabriel. It is indeed unfortunate that so many workers never know the pleasure of engaging in a subtle craft such as you and my father have mastered. I agree that too much work is merely repetitive and tedious."

Gabriel's eyes shifted as he realized that Belle's own

sewing was not far removed from what he had characterized. It also flooded back to him that she communed with Lily during her solitary labor. The Endicotts were old friends, and Archie had confided this to him.

"It is simply sad," said Gabriel.

"Perhaps," said Archie, "if our partnership lets us see the factory rooms, we can be of some comfort to the workers."

"Yes," said Belle, "and help ensure their fair treatment."

She extended a hand. "Dear Mr. Gabriel, you have inspired us. Thank you ever so much."

Gabriel's face twisted between warmth and shame. He squeezed Belle's hand, then reached for Archie's.

"Well, all my best wishes on your endeavor," he said. "I do advise caution. One cannot be too careful with these men of business."

"We shall be as wise as serpents," said Belle. "Thank you."

"Now," said Gabriel, "let me place an order for your usual buttons." He emphasized "usual."

"Our old-fashioned buttons," said Archie, tossing what had become a favorite joke.

"Classic," Gabriel amended.

Belle raised her eyebrows in pleasure and exchanged smiles with Archie.

"Classic," they mouthed to each other.

The primary interest of most of their customers was the promised savings from manufactured buttons. Many took no care to hide this and clearly gave no thought to the implications for the messengers.

"Cheaper buttons?" said a tailor named Merrell. "Hallelujah! Every bit helps. Glad to hear it!"

"We are happy for you," said Belle. Archie

appreciated how she suppressed her smile.

"When does this begin?" Merrell blundered on. "Are the cheaper buttons available now? Where do you stand with the order that I have with you?"

"The factory can take orders immediately," said Belle.

"They can deliver the same as I have already ordered?"

Ebenezer had provided an assortment of samples, so Archie and Belle were able to show what was available from the factory. Merrell seized on one item.

"How much is this?" he said. Belle named the cost.

"Gracious sakes, yes!" Merrell said. "I want a gross."

"Very well," said Belle. "We will cancel your order with us and communicate your new order to the factory."

"When will I get them?"

"Tomorrow," said Archie.

"Who will bring them by?"

"A representative of the owner."

"Isn't that what you are?"

Simultaneously, Archie answered yes and Belle answered no. They looked at each other.

"Well, yes, today we are representatives," Belle said. "In a manner of speaking."

"I'll watch for whoever comes by," Merrell said.

"Thank you for your business and for this order," said Belle.

"I'm glad for the savings," said Merrell.

After they left, several doors away from Merrell's shop and well out of his hearing, Archie said, "He'll miss us."

"Obviously," said Belle.

twenty-two

A business decision

Along these lines, the early days of their transition into Ebenezer's fledgling business went very well. Classic Buttons, as Archie and Belle began to refer to their shop, gained more orders than they had seen in ages. Belle delightedly told Lily all about it.

Ebenezer's completing the setup of the factory? This, too, went well.

Hiring die makers? It went well.

Hiring sculptors, production managers, machine attendants? These all went very well.

And yet, though he took care never to show it, Ebenezer grew ever more anxious. This expensive undertaking put his entire savings at risk, as well as bank loans and private investments. He had no partners, insisting on being the one managing director. He slept little and paced much. Actually, he no longer slept at all. He simply went to his flat when he felt the last of his strength draining, dropped from exhaustion, regained consciousness after a time and began again.

Even as the undertaking quickly took pleasing shape, he felt his own suspicions grow. Why was all of this working? As confident as he was, he could not escape a sense of dread. Was the universe executing a malicious trick, conniving to lull him into ease before dropping a mountain on his head? Ebenezer could not rest in peace. He stood in the light and looked for shadows.

To make matters worse—that is, better—hiring the six sales representatives and narrowing them as described, from five to four to three—this went exceedingly well. A surprising development even helped Ebenezer hit upon a further improvement in operations. This transpired as follows.

With coaxing from two of the representatives, Jonson and Sincello, Ebenezer decided to release the third, Gordimer, whose orders rapidly fell behind those of his colleagues. Gordimer was stunned by his dismissal, which came privately in Ebenezer's office. Decades older than the remaining pair of salesmen, who were somewhat older than Ebenezer himself, Gordimer's appearance reminded Ebenezer of his despised schoolmaster from long ago, though Gordimer's manner was warm and kindly, something that surely aided his selling efforts. All of this swirled in Ebenezer's mind as he imparted his decision. Gordimer leaned back heavily in his chair.

"You will retain only two salesmen, then, not three after all?"

"Correct," said Ebenezer.

This was true for the time being, though barely. Ebenezer had engaged a third representative on a provisional basis. His name was Usstin, and he happened to be a mutual acquaintance of Jonson and Sincello, who had not known each other before coming to work for Ebenezer. Each had praised Usstin as a mentor in the area of selling. This reminded Ebenezer of his own tutelage by Fezziwig, and he took a meeting with Usstin in his preferred tavern. Ebenezer found the man to be magnetic and persuasive, and he had no doubt of Usstin's potential to surpass even the engaging Gordimer. He made it clear that Usstin had one week in which to prove himself, and his newest employee readily agreed.

Ebenezer left the meeting somewhat intoxicated, not from an evening grog but from the new dynamic that had presented itself. He had meant to conclude the competition that gave him three salesmen, but now he realized that it could continue indefinitely, and in all areas of his business. He resolved to regularly interview promising candidates for positions and offer them provisional employment if a particular employee should fall behind others in that same role. His business would rise due to an ongoing Struggle to Survive, as Belle had termed it. Stronger employees would continually replace the weaker.

But to return to Gordimer's question: Ebenezer had indeed reduced his sales force to two. Usstin would begin on the morrow, but this was no business of Gordimer's.

"May I have a moment, sir, to sit and take this in?" Gordimer asked.

"A moment, yes."

Gordimer shook his head as from a blow. He even dazedly raised a hand to his jaw.

"I must compliment Jonson and Sincello," he said, "since they came to acquire significantly more orders than I was able to. The three of us enjoyed comparing notes, both with each other and with you in our collective meetings, and my impression was that each of us was similarly productive."

"This was so until recently," said Ebenezer. "The figures tell the story." He placed a finger on his ledger without turning it for Gordimer to see. "Their orders rapidly climbed, while yours did not. I had to address the inequity."

Gordimer grimaced and nodded, his brow wrinkled in consternation. Finally he managed a smile, clapped his knees and stood. "Well, it is a good reminder that life can surprise, and that things can turn around in a wink." He extended a hand to Ebenezer. "It has been a pleasure to briefly be associated with you, Mr. Scrooge. You are creating an impressive business that I am sorry to leave. I offer all best wishes. Thank you for the opportunity."

Ebenezer took care to look Gordimer in the eye and shake his hand firmly. The man had learned a hard lesson.

"I'll walk out with you."

"Kind of you, sir."

This was not merely a gesture of camaraderie, however. Ebenezer had an important errand. He put the sales ledger under his arm and reached for his hat. After tipping the latter a final time to Gordimer, he continued on to the bank.

twenty-three

A plea

Ebenezer had become a familiar figure to James McHugh, his young account manager at the nearby branch of National Provincial. Fezziwig had introduced them, sometimes to McHugh's chagrin, since Ebenezer regularly crossed the threshold of his office to beg a larger line of credit. He was forever pressing into McHugh's hands his sales ledger to demonstrate the healthy income that supported his pledges to pay back what he borrowed.

"Not again," McHugh muttered under his breath as his eye caught Ebenezer's signature rapid march along the street. But he showed only a smile as the young entrepreneur burst in toward him.

"McHugh," Ebenezer said without preamble, "I must have a new machine."

"Good morning to you as well, Mr. Scrooge."

"What? Oh, yes, fine morning. Better than you know." To provide illustration, he flopped open his ledger.

"Sales rising still?"

"Soaring." Ebenezer pointed out the relevant figures. McHugh's eyebrows lifted. "Ah."

"We cannot keep up. I need that new machine, and I must act quickly. I cannot have Reedison buy it first."

"I have not heard you mention Reedison before."

"That is because I was more worried about Shapleigh, but now Shapleigh is gone."

"Gone?"

"Dead, man! Don't you listen when I give you news of the trade?"

"Oh, yes, you did tell me, and now I recall your eyeing his equipment. I beg your pardon."

"I will gladly exchange my pardon for a loan."

"Noted."

McHugh did literally take notes about Shapleigh and his possibly-obtainable equipment, even as Ebenezer pressed for yet another boost to his line of credit. Ultimately, however, he secured only McHugh's promise to study the matter with his colleagues.

"We must not make the mistake of overextending you, Mr. Scrooge," McHugh said as he ushered him out.

"Nor of underextending the bank," said Ebenezer. "Do not let my gain be your loss."

"Much to avoid," said McHugh as he closed the door.

"Much to avoid," Ebenezer muttered as he returned to his office. "Humbug."

twenty-four

Elaborate justification

The machine that Ebenezer coveted had served a business that formed only months before his own, but that company had already shuttered due to the owner's death from a sudden onset of bronchitis. Ebenezer had known and observed the gentleman, Curtis Shapleigh, and he felt, if not bereaved, something of a kinship with another in the same burgeoning industry, and Shapleigh had also been working tirelessly. Ebenezer knew this in minute detail because of, to put it simply, spies.

Those who gave him information about Shapleigh were the man's own employees, who sought out Ebenezer as a competitor who might be pay for minor bits of news. At first, Ebenezer vehemently shunned these overtures, but he changed his mind when Shapleigh's men informed him that Shapleigh had paid some of them to apply for jobs with Scrooge so they could see Scrooge's factory. Hearing this, Scrooge readily parted with a few coins to stay abreast of relevant developments.

He justified such efforts as private journalism. This was worthy reporting within a slim range of interests for an audience consisting solely of himself. What was wrong with that? Was it not just another form of enterprise?

Of course, there were complications. These "reporters" cared only about the story at hand, not the need to maintain accuracy over time. In other words, alleyway correspondents could not be trusted. They were all too ready to bend the truth for profit.

Thus, Ebenezer had to obtain verification from multiple inside sources, for additional payment. And he learned to engage outside emissaries. For instance, after Ebenezer first learned that Shapleigh could not shake a persistent cough, he hired a neighborhood runabout to linger outside the business until Shapleigh emerged and tell what he saw.

"I thought he would never exit, Mr. Scrooge," the boy said, "but finally, finally he came out after midnight. And was he ever moving slow, sir. Walking like he was in mud, all bent over and wheezing. Pitiful it was, sir."

This did the story of Shapleigh's demise reach the Scrooge Chronicle, as it were, before the general public. It was vital for Ebenezer to recast these activities as innovative journalism. For if there was one thing he could not abide it was industrial espionage.

twenty-five

Deplored practice

Ebenezer was not alone in this. Multitudes in Britain had been scandalized in recent decades as expatriates helped light the wildfire spread of textile manufacturing in that difficult cousin of nations, the United States. The most famous of these turncoats, as they were considered, was Samuel Slater, "Slater the Traitor," who left home soil at the age of 21, flouting the ban on emigration of skilled textile workers to recreate Richard Arkwright's wondrous water-powered mills in the American state called Rhode Island. Fezziwig had acquainted Ebenezer with the story of Slater and received a one-word response.

"Perfidious!"

Fezziwig's chuckle drew Ebenezer's face tight.

"Forgive me, Ebenezer, but such a word!"

"None other will suffice for such calculating, contemptible—"

"Industrious, intrepid ..."

"Intrepid!"

"Slater was a clever boy from Belper. Good on him, I say."

Ebenezer's mouth was agape. "How can you possibly condone such, such— "

"Perfidy?"

Ebenezer stood in protest. Fezziwig waved in mollification. "I'm sorry, son. I could not help myself. Please forgive me and tell me why you feel so strongly about this."

Ebenezer glowered but resumed sitting. "It's treason! Aiding our enemies? Stealing inventions and slinking abroad illegally? How could anyone defend this?"

"Some see it as fair turnabout."

Ebenezer's brow wrinkled in question.

"What I mean, lad," said Fezziwig, "is that Britain did the same to Italy, over a hundred years ago. A chap named John Lombe connived his way into an Italian silk mill and made technical drawings at night. The Italians discovered this, and Lombe barely made it out on a vessel chased by a warship. He based new spinning machines on his drawings, and his mill exploded with success. Sadly, he paid with his life."

"What?! What happened?"

"His factory was infiltrated by a woman. The King of Sardinia sent her to beguile and poison him. Lombe was dead before he saw thirty."

Ebenezer's face darkened.

"So yes, lad, espionage is serious. But it happens in all directions."

"Have you encountered it personally?"

"I have not. But then the warehousing business does not involve complex machinery nor new technology. Little would be learned from skulking in here after hours. Or striding in during!" He added this last with a laugh. "Other than to lift with one's legs rather than with one's back. And the power of simple perseverance."

Ebenezer made a mental note to guard against

espionage if he entered a business dependent on complex machinery or new technology. Now he was in exactly that situation.

twenty-six

Safeguards in action

Scrooge Button Manufacturing employed careful defenses. Ebenezer placed his manufacturing equipment behind walls and posted a guard at the room's entry.

He was proud of his "button password" system. He gave instructions to set aside supplies of particular buttons in boxes labeled with particular dates. The first order of every day's operations was for each entering employee to hand over the button of the day. A careful record was kept of the ingoing and outgoing unique specimens.

The day came when a woman attempting the employee entrance had been found out for lacking the correct button, nor even being aware of the practice. It was the day after McHugh put off Ebenezer's request for credit for the new machine.

Using a route that shielded the manufacturing floor, the guard took the young woman to Ebenezer's office. She marched in head high. Ebenezer did not offer a seat.

"What is your name, Miss?" he said.

"Lottie," she said defiantly.

"Surname?"

"Edward."

"What did you have in mind coming here, Miss Edward?"

"Workin'"

"What type of work?"

"Why, makin' buttons, o' course."

"And what do you know of making buttons?"

"How hard can it be? Standin' at a machine. Or sittin'. I can do either."

"Where were you yesterday, Miss Edward?"

"Yesterday?" Her eyes slid to and fro. "I was, er—"

"How did you know how to get here?"

"Here?"

"This building."

"A gent'leman tol' me, he did."

"He told you there might be work for you here?"

"He did."

"How did he know?"

"Said you were flamin' busy, rollin' out buttons like rain."

"How did he know that?"

"He seen your carts come out full o' boxes."

"What time of day?"

"He seen your carts come out at— "

"No, pardon me, that's not what I meant. What time of day did he tell you these things?"

"Oh. Early afte'noon."

"Yesterday?"

"Righto."

"What time of day?"

"I just said. Early afte'noon."

"No, pardon me. What time of day did he say that my carts roll out?"

After a beat, Lottie said, "See here, you're just tryin' to confuse me."

"How so?"

"Goin' back and forth about times o' day, once about the carts and then about me speakin' to the gent'leman."

"Mr. Reedison?"

"Yes, Mister Ree— " She stopped herself, but it was too late.

"You may go, Miss Edward."

"You tricked me!"

"And you tried to steal information from me."

"See here, I— "

"That's enough, Miss," said the guard. "Out you go."

"I do have a final question for you, Miss Edward," said Ebenezer.

"More trickery!"

"Nothing of the sort. Only this: Do you know the penalty for espionage?"

"Espi— what now?"

"Spying."

"I di'nt do no spying!"

"You didn't get to, you mean," said the guard.

"You stay out'n this!" spat Lottie.

"If you were to spy," said Ebenezer, "you ought to know the penalty."

"Why? What is it?"

"Ask about. You won't like what you hear."

The guard showed Lottie to the exit. Ebenezer sat and with a slow breath extended his hands and pressed them flat on his desk.

twenty-seven

Flustered

He was both pleased and rattled.

His security measures had worked, including the methodical questioning that had tilted Lottie off balance. He felt tipsy from the surge in his blood that had inspired his final ominous warning about the penalty for spying. This had been pure bluff, since he did not know the answer himself, but he felt certain that Lottie would inquire hither and thither. Hopefully, she would receive a range of foreboding responses that would prompt her to abandon skulduggery and urge others to do the same.

Ebenezer found the thought satisfying but sour. He loathed such additions to his already-demanding everyday—and everynight—work. He had a bottomless appetite for good, honest effort, but no taste whatever for contending with cheats and scoundrels.

"Ah, Fezziwig," he sighed.

Wait, had he spoken aloud? His eyes darted about. Had anyone seen him talking to himself? He swiveled his wheeled chair toward the corner so as to appear in sober contemplation, even as he squeezed shut his eyes.

What had flooded upon him was not only the thought of his old master, but a craving for the simplicity of his former role as an all-around assistant who was frequently diverted from ledger books for tasks such as unloading wagons or sweeping floors. Those were good days. The freedom! The ease! The memory put him on the verge of weeping.

This was not the first time for this mental journey. In his few moments of repose, Ebenezer often found himself drifting in imagination to the tiny but tidy desk where he had methodically marshalled the comings and goings of property in Fezziwig's warehouse, as well as the flows of money through expenses and income. Accounting thoroughly agreed with him. His fingers could dance through ledger tables like Liszt's upon keys. With one glance at a page, Ebenezer could seize upon an error or crucial pattern. It was his gift.

He did and did not miss his earlier life. He would still do exactly as he had done—strike out on his own in a business—but undeniably he felt a melancholy for what he had left behind. That part of his past was a refuge. Somewhere to go amid turmoil. A place of peace.

A place of peace. That gave him a new thought. Then indecision rippled.

Should I? he mused. *Is it proper?*

He quickly decided in the affirmative, rose and reached for his hat. And as he did dozens of times each day, he slipped his hand into his vest pocket and found the red button—that is, he found me.

He nodded to his plant manager on his way out and was soon striding briskly across the cobblestones.

twenty-eight

A spirited discussion

Mother! Must you interrupt me?

Certainly I must, if you insist on prattling on about the button business at a time like this.

Prattling on. Pffft.

At a time like this. Ordinarily I live for your prattling.

Live for it. I'll pardon the expression.

As always.

At a time like this?

You know what I mean.

I am sure I do not.
I am sure you do.
You refer to … ?
I will not play your game, Daughter.
I will not play yours, Mother.
As you wish.

For a time, they sewed in silence, Lily ethereally and Belle materially, until the latter lowered her work.

Oh, all right, Mother.
Yes, Dear?
You wish to hear about Ebenezer Scrooge.
And you wish to tell me.
In fact, I do.
Then do.
We have been bustling ever since he appeared, Mother. So many orders! Father could not be happier.
Could he not?
Happier about business, I mean.
I take your meaning, Daughter.
I am sure you do. He does miss you.
I know, and I miss him. But tell me more about his missing me.
What about Ebenezer, Mother? Suddenly he can wait?
He can wait. You were saying that your father said … ?
Let me think. I want to use his exact words from the other day, when we both worked so late to keep up. Oh, yes, he said, (Belle inserted a sad sigh here), "I miss your mother. We could really use another pair of hands right now."

Lily giggled, and Belle along with her, until Lily spoke softly.

How is he?

Tired, but he has been saying, "Oh, to always be tired like this." From having so much work to do.

Well, money helps. He worries about how you will get on when he joins me.

May that time tarry.

Agreed. He will be with me again soon enough, and then forever. I will be patient.

When that time comes, I will be fine.

Financially, I have no doubt. You can always take care of yourself.

How else will I not be fine?

You will be lonely.

I will not.

Says the unmarried woman.

Says the unmarried woman, yes.

Speaking of which …

Ah, here we are again.

Speaking of which … we have yet to begin discussing Ebenezer.

We have begun.

No, because you steered the talk, once again, to business.

Ebenezer and business are the same thing.

He is not business.

He is our employer.

And …

And that is all.

That is not all.

Of course it is.

May I illustrate how it is not?

Impossible, but I'm sure you will try.

My illustration is Mr. Merrell.

Ha! The tailor?

Indeed, he of the blunt charms.

What about the bluntly charming Mr. Merrell?
Better put, charmingly blunt.
What about Mr. Merrell, Mother?
Is your relationship with him only business?
Certainly!
The same as with young Mr. Scrooge?
Exactly the same.
Oh, that sounds convincing.
Well, not exactly.
Aha!
Because Mr. Merrell is a customer. Ebenezer is our employer. But both relationships are simply business.
Transactional.
Transactional only. Only transactional.
Which transactions do you prefer?
Mother ...
Those with Mr. Merrell or those with Ebenezer?
They are fundamentally identical.
Your anticipation for each is identical.
Yes. If there is any anticipation, it is about getting paid.
In each case.
In each case.
There are no other rewards.
None.
I see.
I'm glad you see. Are we finished?
We still have not begun.
Mother, honestly! Ebenezer is our employer. That is the end of it.

Lily raised her chin and closed her eyes. Belle could not suppress a tight smile. Lily might as well have announced, "I am burrowing yet deeper into your spirit"—surpassing even their ordinary celestial

communion (if it could ever be termed ordinary). Soon
enough, Lily placed upon Belle an all-seeing gaze.

That is not the end of it, Dearest.

Belle's chin quivered.

Oh, all right. But I must regard it as the end, Mother.
To do otherwise would not be proper. Nor wise. I must
not cloud any decisions that Father and I make, or that
Ebenezer makes.

Any monetary decisions.

Yes. It is a matter of survival. I do enjoy Ebenezer,
and over these months he has drawn my heart. I do
believe that I have special insight into him—that I can
read him as if he were a book written in a language that I
alone speak. I do sense that he has a sharp interest in me,
and a tender regard. He is particularly sensitive regarding
my conversations with you.

As one would hope.

Yes, so understanding of something so unusual. Not
at all judgmental, only keenly interested and properly
inquisitive. I might even say fascinated. In turn I admire
his energy and initiative and attention to detail. I find his
earnestness endearing, and he makes my heart swell with
hope.

How marvelous.

But he does not inspire only hope in me, Mother. I
fear for him.

What do you fear?

I fear his collapse, ultimately, from working too hard
or from disappointment. Father and I talk about this,
because he sensed the same thing in Ebenezer from his
very first visit. It is clear to me how much his work means
to him. He is entwined in his own doing, and I feel

certain that it is how he measures his own worth as a person. But businesses fail, even those with the strongest and most intelligent and most determined at the helm. And that is how I see Ebenezer: Strong, sharp, eminently able to command an enterprise. But not superhuman. I fear what will happen to him if circumstances become adverse. I fear that it will be a blow to his very soul.

I am sorry to hear that, Dearest. It is worrisome that he strives so fiercely. That invites pain and loss atop loss.

What can I do for him, Mother?

What have you thought of doing?

I try to be kind. When I speak to him, I purposely address the man, not the employer—whenever it is not a matter of business. It is a shift that I make in my mind. When I greet him, at that moment I do not work for him. I greet him as a friend, and I hope a dear friend. I do try to modulate my fervor, though, so as to … to …

So as not to appear a tease.

Exactly, Mother! Wait, you know exactly … ?

Do not be surprised or scandalized, Dearest. I know what it is to be aware of one's effect on another. Why, one of the button customers—But no, I will not discuss that.

Mother! You can't leave me hanging like that!

Of course I can. No more need be said. I simply perfected modulation, to use your term.

Were you ever in danger?

Was I? Hm, let us say that I felt a tension.

What did you do?

I attracted a dog.

Muggins!

Yes, homely old Muggins, who hung about our door waiting to be fed. I had observed that this troublesome customer did not care for canines. He gave them a wide berth.

Oh, Mother, now I know who you mean!

Lily made a small, tight sound of annoyance.

Him! With the drooping mustache! What was his name?

Oh, never you mind. He is not worth discussing. But now you know. I went out of my way to find a formidable dog on the street, and there he was, the big old bear, and I started to feed him, so he took up his post outside the shop, and you named him Muggins.

I did? I always thought that Father did.

No, you did. You were just too young to remember.

Huh. So that's where he came from.

That's where he came from. And thankfully Mr. Mustache stopped coming around.

How wonderfully awful, and awfully wonderful— because it all led to Muggins.

That sums up life with men, my dear. No, not quite. It can also be awfully awful. Never wonderfully wonderful.

Even with Father?

Ah, Archie. How I love him. I must say: He and I are a perfect match. Except in life span.

Belle could not help laughing at this.

But he and I were often at odds. You might not recall.

I don't! I don't recall so much as a cross word between you.

Cross words, no. Archie Endicott, raise his voice? Never. But that can be vexing in its own way. "Show some excitement, Dear Man! Get upset! Laugh from your belly!" But no.

Not Father.

"And can't you please talk a bit faster? Why do I finish your sentences? Because you speak so slowly that I might not live to hear the last word!"

Mother, you are awful!

I am.

Wonderfully awful.
I sound like a man!

Belle chuckled, but this soon subsided, and she gained a far-away look.

I know what you are doing, Dear Belle.
Oh?
You are thinking of Ebenezer.
Perhaps.
And calculating where life with him would fall, between awful and wonderful.
Ugh, I hate when you see right through me.
We've already ruled out wonderfully wonderful.
And it would not be awfully awful.
Are you quite sure?
Mother!
Belle.
Why, how— Why would you ever think that? Based on everything that I've told you? Ebenezer is thoughtful and sensitive and …
And ambitious and exacting, you have said.

Belle had told Lily how Ebenezer thoroughly questioned such details as why Archie and she chose this or that material or supplier or technique. He was clearly seeking to understand each decision and gain every cost advantage, both in the immediate transaction and in the ultimate suitability of the product for customers. The close view and long views, he called them.

But discipline and attention to detail are important qualities for business.
Yes, but a home is not a business, and a marriage is not merely a legal partnership.

It is good to have high standards. I do as well.

And it is good to be decisive. But many a husband trusts his own decisions and his own perspective above all others.

Many a wife as well.

And many a daughter.

And many mothers.

A beat passed before Lily spoke.

Am I vexing you, Dear?

To be honest, Mother, yes. I am wounded that you would even suggest that Ebenezer is awfully awful. He is not.

I do not agree that I said that.

You did!

Well, perhaps I did brush against that meaning. Forgive me.

Hmpf.

I meant to get at the broader matter of life with a man, rather than this specific man. With any man, there are dynamics that come into play—

Such as being overly exacting.

Such as being exacting, and it is worth considering when exacting becomes overly exacting.

But that is already your conclusion.

It is not my conclusion to make, Dearest. It is you who would decide. I merely wish you to regard marriage with open eyes.

Marriage, yes! You have made it clear that you have already concluded that Ebenezer and I will marry! Rather, you have concluded our engagement, not to mention initiating it, and you already have me married to that awfully awful, overly-exacting young man.

Belle, sweetheart, you are agitated.

And you are exasperating!

I am not saying that your young man is fundamentally, to the core, absolutely awfully awful.

He is not my young man!

Is he not?

Is he not awfully awful?

Please, let's discuss this another time.

Why wait? Don't you want to tell me more now about how awful Ebenezer is?

Yes, definitely another time.

I'll be sure to tell him what you think.

He'll be all the more intrigued about his future mother-in-law.

And relieved that he need never face her!

Lily was silent.

Oh, Mother, I'm sorry. I—

Be well, my love. Give your father a hug for me. I'll watch for you another time.

Mother—

But Lily faded away.

The button shop swirled into being around Belle, and she found her hand being pressed in concern. She knew at once that this was not the touch of her father, but it was as soft and tender.

Her eyes met a concerned gaze. It was Ebenezer.

twenty-nine

An invitation

"I am sorry," Belle said. "I should not have said that."

"It's all right, Dear Belle." It was a reassuring hush.

"But I— She thinks—"

Belle trailed off as she came back to herself and to the hard edges and glare of the shop.

Ebenezer didn't hear Mother, she thought. *No one else hears her, not even—*

No sooner had Belle thought of her father than she discovered that he was standing beside Ebenezer. Even as she realized this, Ebenezer rose, and Archie replaced him in the chair.

Belle knew that Archie saw it all in her eyes—that she'd had an upsetting exchange with her mother.

"Are you quite all right, Dearest?" he said.

"Yes. I— " Her mind felt clouded, but she was aware of muting herself in Ebenezer's presence. That would not do.

She looked straight into Archie's eyes and squeezed his hands.

"I am fine, Father, thank you. Mother sends her regards. And this."

She gently drew Archie to his feet and wrapped him in a hug. Belle felt a delicious relaxation in her father, but when he leaned back, tension remained in his face. She squeezed his hands.

"Ebenezer," Belle said in greeting, reaching toward him.

"Belle," he said, stepping forward to lightly grasp her hand.

"I'm afraid you saw a sight just now. I do apologize."

"No need whatever. I only hope you are not troubled."

"How kind of you. I suppose that a walk would do me good. Would you mind coming along?"

Belle was surprised by her own request but managed to keep this from her face. Not so for Ebenezer. She saw delight ripple through him.

"Certainly," he said. "If you are feeling steady."

"Steady enough," she said. She turned toward Archie. "Just a short break, Father."

He beamed warmly. "Make it a good long one."

As she was walking ahead of Ebenezer out the door that he had opened for her, it registered: *He called me Dear Belle.*

thirty

An admission

"Do you have a few moments for me to tell you about my mother?" Belle said as they strolled.

"It would be my honor. Take all the time you like."

"I've never given you a proper explanation of my ... visits with her."

"Whatever you care to say or not say is perfectly proper."

"The truth is, I don't know wh— "

Suddenly a moan broke from Belle. She swayed, steadying herself against Ebenezer's arm. Bracing her, he turned a degree to shield her from view. She loosed a heart-rending keen.

"I'm so— sor— " But she could not finish speaking.

"Perfectly proper," Ebenezer repeated softly. "Take all the time you like."

Belle hooked his elbow with her hand and steered him into a passage between two buildings. The slow traverse to the end would provide some seclusion for composing herself.

"I do apologize—again—Ebenezer. I was going to say

that I do not know whether my mother is actually there, present, in these interludes. It pains me to admit this— wounds me deeply, to be frank. It is like losing her again." Her voice quavered, but she pressed on. "I can be sure of nothing, because even though I talk with Mother all the while we are together, Father assures me that I only sew the entire time and never appear to interact."

"That has been my observation as well, each time that I happened to be present—was fortunate to be present—including today," said Ebenezer. "Your only movements are in your hands and your head as you turn toward your materials and in your eyes as you sight them. But as you describe, it is still evident that you inhabit a different plane of experience."

"There, yet not there."

"Exactly."

"So I gather. I recognize that these conversations might be completely fabricated in my mind. And yet they are as real to me as this moment with you. It has even made me question the nature of reality itself. How much of what we see around us is really real? And how much do we create?"

"Learned scholars ask similar questions. I have read them in books."

"I have seen them also, but what have you read?"

"So very much. It is hard to know where to begin."

"Start anywhere."

Ebenezer's hand was on the button in his pocket, and inspiration struck him.

thirty-one

An illustration

"Very well, something does come to mind. This is an illustration from a book whose title I do not recall, but I could find it in one of my notebooks. Say that two people are in a room ...

"May we call them Belle and Ebenezer?"

"Certainly. Ebenezer has a button, Belle does not."

"Hmpf."

"In the room are a basket and a box. Ebenezer places the button in the basket and is suddenly called away. In his absence, Belle— "

"Puts the button in the box!"

"Oh, have you already read this example?"

"No, but it seems like something Belle would do."

"Doesn't it? Presently, Ebenezer returns. Where does he look for the button?"

"In the basket, of course."

"But we know it's not there."

"But he doesn't know."

"Why doesn't he know?"

"Because he wasn't there when it was moved. He proceeds from what is in his mind."

"Even though it is incorrect."

"But he doesn't know that it's incorrect."

"And there you have it."

"Have what?"

"The point of the illustration is that the mind can hold a false belief."

"And your point is that my mother is a false belief?"

"No, no, indeed not. Or at least, that is not why I offered the illustration. You yourself have already said that your perception of your mother might be a false belief."

"Yes."

"The book I was reading did use this story to illustrate a false belief. But I came away seeing it as illustrating a true belief. Because Ebenezer has every reason to believe the button is in the basket. He put it there himself. That is truth."

"It is his truth."

"Exactly so—his truth."

"Until it is proven false."

"Until it is proven false."

"And this relates to my holding my mother in my mind?"

"Does it not?"

"Does it?"

"Your mother is without doubt in your mind, as surely as the button is in the basket. You have found her there. You have every reason to expect to find her there again. That is truth."

"My truth."

"Your truth."

"Until it is proven false."

"How could it ever be proven false?"

Belle was struck by this thought, and she halted walking.

"You are saying that only I have access to my own mind."

"Certainly. As is the case with each of us."

"And what I have found to be true is true."

"Truly."

"But … is it real?"

Ebenezer paused and extended his hand. Belle looked at him. Ebenezer nodded, and Belle placed her fingers on his.

"Is my hand real?"

"Yes."

"How do you know?"

"I feel it."

"You perceive it through the sense of touch."

"Yes."

"Your perception is what makes it real."

"Yes."

"Is your mother real?"

"Yes. No. I don't know. By the test you have given, yes. I experience her. I perceive her through the sense of — It is not a physical sense."

"Is all reality physical?"

"Surely not."

"I agree. For example ..." Ebenezer looked off and drew in a breath, seeming to settle on a decision.

"For example: Love."

thirty-two

Feelings revealed

"That is a good example," Belle said. She suddenly realized that Ebenezer still held her hand.

"Do you feel it?" he said.

"Your hand?"

"My love. For you, Dear Belle."

Belle stopped breathing. The entire world hung suspended.

"I do."

"And you? Is there any chance that you harbor love ... for me?"

"I believe ... I do."

Ebenezer removed his hat. "My precious Belle, I— "

She touched his sleeve to forestall him, as he had not noticed an old woman just then tottering past. She eyed the pair suspiciously. Ebenezer reflexively reached up to doff his hat, finding, of course, that it was already in his hands. So his act of courtesy became a sort of awkward pushing of his hat toward the woman. He realized that he might seem to be shooing her away. And indeed, with an expression mingling surprise and irritation, she gave the couple a wider berth as she moved along.

Grinning at this, Belle once again hooked Ebenezer by the arm and drew him into the passage between buildings.

"I was going to say, Dear Belle, that— "

He looked at her, at a loss for words, and they came to a stop.

"Well, I don't know exactly what to say, but I want to say something."

"Something about the two of us?"

"Yes."

"Is it a … suggestion?" She took care to avoid the word "proposal."

"Yes."

"Regarding— ?"

"Do you suppose that we two— that you and I— that is, might we— Oh, I am doing so badly at this."

"Just say it, Ebenezer."

He drew a breath.

"Belle Endicott, would you ever, ever, possibly … that is, might you consider … becoming my wife?"

"I must confess, I have considered it. The idea even— " She cut herself off, then decided she would keep no secrets from her young man. "The idea even came up earlier today, between Mother and me."

"It did?"

"It did."

"May I ask how the idea happened to arise?"

"She mentioned you. But I saw afterward that I had led her to mention you."

"May I ask how?"

"By showing my interest in you."

"May I ask— Oh, forgive me for repeating myself."

"She noted that I spoke highly of you."

"May I— " But he bit his tongue rather than remain in this rut of repetition. He fell silent and could only beseech Belle with his eyes. With a rush of affection, she wished that she might forever hold in her mind that particular composition of Ebenezer's features, mingling so many emotions.

Finally he managed to speak. "It warms my heart to hear that you spoke highly of me."

"And you warm my heart, Ebenezer. You are remarkably kind to Father and me, and stimulating to talk to. I eagerly anticipate your visits, and I admire all that you do in business."

"How kind of you to say. Sometimes I wonder if I am up to it. But I will press on."

"I know you will."

They had once again reached the end of the passage that they had entered.

Ebenezer looked up the street to his right and then back to Belle's eyes.

"Which way now?" he asked.

thirty-three

An agreement

Belle started to ponder and then burst out, "Oh! I have not yet answered your question."

"Ah, indeed." His tone was mild but told Belle that he had noticed her failure to reply and had been waiting hopefully.

She swung him about, and they once again walked toward the far end of the passage.

"As I said, I have considered what you suggest. But that was idle speculation in the absence of actual possibility. Do you see what I mean?"

"I do. I suppose I was engaging in much the same."

"Daydreaming."

"Nights as well, for me."

"Ah! But now, it seems fair to say, there is indeed an actual possibility."

"That is my fervent desire."

"And we may both consider it, for a time."

"I will be thinking of nothing else."

"Nor I." She gave his arm a light squeeze.

"Do you have a thought for how long to …"

"Consider?"

"Yes. And when we should ..."

"Confer?"

"Yes."

"Do you?"

"I will utterly defer to you, Dear Belle. Take all the time you like."

"I have no idea what might be proper, but— "

"Whatever you suggest will be most appropriate."

"Then … twenty-four hours? Could you return to the shop at the same time tomorrow?"

"With pleasure."

"The same time as your arrival today—so a bit less than twenty-four hours."

"All the better."

"Agreed then."

They stood for a moment with eyes locked, holding hands.

"Speaking of your coming to the shop today, may I ask why? And how it was that I came awake to find you before me rather than Father?"

"The truth is, you are the reason I went to the shop."

"Oh?"

"I wanted to see you—needed to see you."

"Needed to?"

"You bring me peace, Dear Belle. You lift me from my own mind. You are a light in the darkness. And the world appeared quite dark to me earlier today."

"Oh, my. Do you want to tell me about it?"

"Perhaps another time. It is a trifle—nothing beside what we have been discussing."

"Is it? If it bothered you enough to seek comfort, it matters to me."

"Another time. It is enough that you are near. You put the sun in the heavens." He raised his face to the overcast sky as if drinking in warmth. "Ahhh."

"Even when there is no sun?" she teased.

He dropped his eyes to her again. "You are a shaft of light in my cell, Dear Belle," he said, lightly emphasizing his unforeseen rhyme.

"Your cell!"

"I mean that sometimes I feel imprisoned by my own thoughts. But when I see you, I become interested in your concerns and your experiences. It is freeing."

"How flattering, Ebenezer. You make me feel so …"

"Liberating."

"… important."

"Of highest importance."

"You will make me blush, sir."

He inspected her cheeks. "Your prediction has come true."

She curled her face down. "Told you," she said.

"Forgive me for causing you discomfort. That was not my intention."

"No, I just— I had no idea that you thought of me so."

"I do."

She decided, blushing or not, to look him in the eye. "And I think of you. I have often imagined you at your desk, intently studying whatever is before you, or standing with your employees, giving direction, negotiating with your suppliers. I admire your enterprise, and I marvel at your energy."

"Now it is I who will blush."

She inspected him. "Your prediction has come true."

thirty-four

Ambition examined

They laughed, then Ebenezer fell solemn.

"Thank you for your kind words. I— I just want to do well."

"You will. You are."

"Not just well— I want to live up to my own capabilities. I want to take my own measure. I must confess, Dear Belle, that when I advance my little schemes in commerce, I feel … tall."

"You are tall."

"Tall and wide and immense. I feel able to stand

astride a full block of London. To plant one foot there, and the other one there"—he said this spreading his arms to indicate the opposite ends of the passageway—"and own everything in between." With a light laugh he said, "I own everything in this empty alley."

Belle nodded encouragingly.

"But someday I will own a full block of shops and dwellings. And I will add another block and another, until I straddle all of London. I believe my mind and spirit are large enough for that. Business can make one a giant. With enough study and effort and determination, I can grow and grow and grow. I want to reach my full size, Dear Belle. I do not want to be a little man."

"You are tall now, Ebenezer." Belle put a hand on each of his arms. "I look up to you already, in more ways than one." His expression filled with tenderness. Gently, he moved his hands toward her shoulders and drew her in. Her mouth tilted up. They kissed.

"Thank you, Dear Belle, for believing in me."

"I do. I believe you will do all you have said."

"That means a great deal."

"But I want you to know, Ebenezer Scrooge: I love you as you are. I do not only admire you—I like you. I enjoy you. I take delight in your mind and your spirit."

Ebenezer swallowed and looked at the ground.

"And your sensitivity," Belle continued. "Look at you, crumpling under compliments." She gently reached up to wipe at the moisture beneath his eyes. He submitted meekly, like a boy to his mother.

"You do not need to grow. And for me you cannot. In my eyes, you are as tall as you will ever be. Success will not add nor failure subtract. I have no doubt that you will become immensely wealthy, but that will not change my regard for you. Grow if it will make you happy, if it is your sport. But for no other reason."

Ebenezer remained still and finally spoke quietly. "Success would make us more secure, Dearest, and that is what I want. For you as for myself—far more for you than for me."

"I know you do. I cherish that aim. But more than security itself, Ebenezer, I cherish that you want me to be secure."

"I do."

"I want you, and your efforts, not the results of your efforts. I will admire the outcomes whatever they are."

"I will do my utmost."

"I know you will. Just like Father."

"Yes," Ebenezer said after a slight faltering.

"All of my life, Father has done everything that he could to nurture me, provide for me and protect me. He has not made me wealthy, but I could not be more satisfied nor more secure. I need you to know that that is my standard for love. He has given me his all."

"I intend the same."

"After Mother— after we lost her, Father did his best to become two parents in one. But he has told me that he soon realized that he needed the aid of women to supply those understandings that he could not. He knew that he would not marry again—he knew Mother to be his one and only companion for life—but when we went to church, he made sure to let me linger with other girls and with women, to be around them. That is how we met Mrs. Cratchit. She became like a dear aunt to me, and— "

"Forgive me for interrupting, Dear Belle, but I just realized the time. I'm afraid that I must return to the factory."

"Oh, yes, of course. I need to get back to work as well."

They once again pivoted toward their original entrance into the passage.

"I promise to ask you more about Mrs. Cricket."

"Cratchit."

"Oh, yes, forgive me."

"I look forward to introducing you to her and to her children. Such dears. I think you will be taken by her youngest in particular. He has the most curious interest in numbers."

"Is that so?"

"Yes, dear little Bob Cratchit."

"Bob! A splendid name for a chap with a mind for money."

"Not only money, though. Numbers in general."

"Oh, that is what you said. I confess that I have nearly come to equate numbers and money. Every moment of my day seems a type of accounting: Numbers of employees, machines, spools of thread, buttons produced. All settling into profit or loss."

"Little Bob Cratchit counts for the joy of it, I think. Everything: Windows, dogs on the street, corners in a room, stitches in a seam, his own steps ..."

"I look forward to meeting this lad. I need workers like him."

They were at the door of the shop now. He warmly pressed her hand between his. Each was aware of forgoing a parting kiss, mindful that Archie would be watching them through the shop's front window.

"I will see you in twenty-four hours," Belle said.

"Within twenty-four." Ebenezer smiled and departed.

thirty-five

A father's reaction

Belle took care to compose herself before opening the door to the shop and made an effort to step in blithely.

It was all for naught. Archie was standing when she entered, holding stock still. As soon as she met his expectant gaze, she felt herself crumple.

"Father ... Father, he ..." she said, laughter bubbling through tears. Archie stepped forward to embrace her.

"I know, Blue Bell, I know." She looked a question at him with damp eyes and dabbed at her cheeks with the handkerchief that he offered.

"I knew he would."

"Had he asked you for his blessing?"

"No, I just knew what he was thinking. I could tell. My blessing is all yours, both of you."

Collapsing into her feeling, Belle folded herself to the floor. Archie pulled up his chair, and Belle leaned her head on his leg. Archie stroked her hair and spoke softly.

"I daresay that I knew before he did. His regard for you was in every look and gesture. I have never seen a man treasure you as I do until I saw it in him, as plain as a berry on snow. So perhaps he did ask me for your hand, but without a word. And without a word, I consented. He came in this morning, having suffered some blow in business or life—it was evident from his bleak expression. He was seeking you with his eyes before he cleared the doorway. I came around the counter and steered him to the chair across from you. I could tell that he needed it. He needed you."

"He said the same—that he needs me. How can that be?"

"'It is not good that the man should be alone,'" Archie quoted softly.

"Oh, Father." Belle circled Archie with her arms, and they lingered holding each other.

thirty-six

A revelation

Ebenezer strode from the button shop with more power and purpose than he had ever known. He felt in another world, with this one merely flowing around him. Even sounds were muffled. He heard only the pound of his heart.

All of his desires mingled: His ardor for Belle, his ambition to succeed, his searing resolve for his abilities to be seen. Feeling rose within him like water in a well after a deluge, the column climbing until it overflows the stone cylinder.

The surge of energy carried him back to the bank and his man there, McHugh. As if materializing from the air, it seemed to McHugh, Scrooge appeared once again, speaking as calmly as a kidnapper to his captive.

"I will buy that machine today, McHugh. How much will the bank go in with me? I'll make up the rest."

McHugh composed himself. "I cannot commit the bank further, Mr. Scrooge. It would expose us to too much risk."

"Can you not increase your lien on my property?"

"Why do you even ask? You have every figure in your head. You know as well as I that our lien already encompasses everything you own. If you fall behind on payments, the bank will seize every last asset and button. We are your sole heir and legatee."

"No, there is more." Ebenezer could hardly believe he was saying this, but the pounding at his temples compelled the words.

"More? What do you mean?"

"I own a shop."

"In addition to the factory?"

"Yes and no. It is part of the same enterprise, but I have not mentioned it until now."

"What is this shop?"

"A button-making shop."

"You mean a traditional button-maker? The very antithesis of your factory?"

"Yes, a boutique. It provides customizing capacity, and a secondary line of products."

"Are there physical assets?"

"A building. Equipment. Inventory. As well as customer accounts."

"What is the value?"

Ebenezer did have all of the figures of his business in his head. The market value of the shop was modest, but it would extend his borrowing power just enough for his new purchase. He and McHugh discussed the matter further and quickly reached an agreement. Ebenezer would provide the ledger that showed the value of the shop, now called Classic Buttons, as well as the document that demonstrated his ownership. The bank would extend its lien to include the shop as well as the new equipment that Ebenezer planned to acquire.

He rose. "I'll return at once with the documents. Prepare the agreement for signing and the record of the new deposit in my account. I'll want to take a bank statement to the current owner of the equipment. I'll talk him into a further discount when I show that I can pay immediately in full."

"You are moving quickly, Ebenezer. Are you quite

sure about all of this?"

"Of course I am. It is perfectly clear and necessary. I'll return shortly." With that, he was gone.

thirty-seven

Colleagues confer

McHugh released a breath. He was standing at his desk when a rap sounded on his door.

"You're frowning," said the coworker standing there, propped in the frame.

"I'm musing," said McHugh as he busied himself with the paperwork for Ebenezer.

"About what just happened?" The colleague nodded after Ebenezer's exit.

"Yes."

"What did just happen?"

"Scrooge is digging his hole even deeper."

"Is it a hole? I thought his business was going well."

"It is. Better all the time, it seems. You saw the latest sales figures."

The colleague nodded. McHugh had conferred with him about Scrooge's plan to buy the new machine to increase production.

"Shapleigh undoubtedly knew that his demise would attract this vulture," the man said.

"Scrooge is a rare bird alright."

"Still, seizing an abandoned machine is good business."

"But at a bad time. He is already mortgaged to his crown, as you know."

"You are extending him further? To his top hat?"

"He suddenly produced more collateral. Or so he says. He will be back presently with papers of ownership."

"Ownership of what?"

"An old-fashioned button works."

"Ah, so suddenly he owns the other end of the industry as well?"

"A piece of it, apparently. To satisfy the nostalgic corner of the market, he says."

"Fascinating. Did he say whether— "

"Ask him yourself if you like." McHugh echoed the previous nod. Already, Ebenezer was about to burst back into the bank.

"I shall," said McHugh's visitor, straightening from his lean.

thirty-eight

A strained introduction

Ebenezer fairly sprinted back into McHugh's office. He slowed and scowled when he found that McHugh was occupied, especially because it was this particular conversation partner. Ebenezer disliked the fellow despite having never met him and not even knowing his name—he had only seen him on visits to the bank. Ebenezer had mentally christened him "Door Knocker," the common reference for the man's unfortunate style of facial hair—a wavering thread underlining his bare cheeks and joining wobbly strips on either side of his mouth. This was complemented higher on his head by a cloud of waving wisps and fuzzy eyebrows, one of which

Ebenezer always found raised askance at his sudden visits.

Door Knocker was about a decade older than Scrooge and McHugh, and Ebenezer read in his hooded eyes and languid bearing that he considered them babes in the woods. Despite his regrettable hair, Door Knocker dressed impeccably. This irked Ebenezer still more. The man had settled into his mind as a figure of ugly ostentation.

"You're frowning," the interloper greeted him.

"Am I?" Ebenezer slid irritated eyes toward McHugh.

"You are," said McHugh.

"Can't imagine why," said Ebenezer. He angled toward McHugh, transparently seeking to have the man to himself.

"Perhaps I'm interrupting," said Door Knocker.

"Perhaps," said Ebenezer over his shoulder.

"I will leave you to your wholesome undertakings," Door Knocker said, emphasizing the "hole" sound for McHugh as their private joke about Scrooge's debt. He turned toward the door.

"Oh, wait," said McHugh. "You had a question for Mr. Scrooge, did you not?"

"Ah, yes," said Door Knocker, turning back. Ebenezer made the most minimal of pivots toward him.

"But first let me introduce you," said McHugh.

With a press of his lips, Ebenezer turned further, as demanded by courtesy, to face Door Knocker.

"Jacob Marley, meet Ebenezer Scrooge. Scrooge, Marley."

The two clasped hands in a test of strength.

"Scrooge," said Marley.

"Marley," said Scrooge.

"Marley supervises my work," said McHugh. He has been with the bank for eight years."

"Capital," said Scrooge.

Marley gave a wolf's smile at this pun.

"Seven years," he corrected McHugh.

"I beg your pardon," said McHugh.

"It just seems longer," suggested Scrooge.

"And you were a clerk, I believe?" said Marley, overpronouncing the title. "With Fezziwig?"

"Managing clerk," noted Scrooge.

"Managing," Marley repeated, as if impressed.

"Supervising, another firm might say."

"Ah, then you understand my role."

"Undoubtedly."

"I aid my colleagues. Stay abreast of their accounts, contribute thoughts, ask questions ..."

"... mingle." Here, Scrooge did his own over-pronouncing.

"I understand that you are pledging new collateral today?"

Ebenezer raised his ownership papers.

"May I?" Marley presented his palm.

"You may." Ebenezer gave him the document.

Marley skimmed the pages. "Classic Buttons," he read aloud. "On Nicholas Street. I know this shop. It belongs to Endicott."

"Did belong."

"Does he know?"

"That I am pledging it?"

"That you own it."

"You see his signature."

"I do. My question remains."

"It seems an insult to his intelligence. He signed."

"It's a compliment. To you and your lawyer. This is expertly drawn."

"There was no lawyer."

"All the more impressive."

"I always take care."

"I'm sure you always do take ... care." Marley delayed the final word, and he made the sentence his parting line. He extended his hand again. Ebenezer took it.

"A pleasure to have met you, sir." He clearly meant it.

"Oh, yes?"

"Oh, yes."

"No further questions?" McHugh said.

"None," said Marley, already turned away. "We may place full confidence in Mr. Scrooge."

"Thank you, Marley," said McHugh.

"Yes," said Ebenezer, "thank you." Marley kept walking but did swivel enough to toss back a nod and raise two fingers in a final farewell.

McHugh leaned forward and whispered. "He likes you! That's impossible!"

"I agree. No one does."

"No no, I mean he doesn't like anyone."

"Not the reverse?"

McHugh huffed a laugh and said quietly, "He always does consider himself the smartest in the room."

"Not this room."

"Of course not," McHugh went along. "Any other, perhaps."

"Not when we enter."

"Or you, at least."

"Don't sell yourself short, man. Look at what wise loans you make."

With that, they returned to business.

thirty-nine

Distracted

Ebenezer bought the new button-making machine with the cash discount, exactly as he had planned. Or rather, as inexactly as he had expected. As typical of business transactions, the purchase presented unique challenges at every step, and it required more time and money than Ebenezer had foreseen. But in a larger sense, this was just what he had foreseen, as he was already becoming a seasoned man of commerce. He resolutely forged ahead.

We will fly through the weeks—nay, let us say months, because two of these, plus a portion of a third, passed before the machine was at full function in Ebenezer's factory beside the other equipment. During this time, he took many walks with Belle, who had indeed become his fiancée.

Shall we skip backward to their reunion to confer on the consideration, as they had referred to it? Of course we shall.

That morning Ebenezer took the greatest care with his grooming and ensemble. He reported to his factory bathed, shaved, plucked, tucked, lotioned, combed, brushed, tailored, pressed and shined. He felt handsome, confident, masterful and utterly impatient, since every matter at hand was merely a tick of the clock that needed to pass before he would depart for Classic Buttons.

He spent the entire morning on his feet so as not to invite a single wrinkle into his clothing. He came to wish that he had a tall desk at which he could stand and work on just such occasions, and he promptly gave specifications to his shop engineer and carpenter for constructing one. For the time being, he made do by having two of his stouter employees stack one table atop another. This left him feeling exposed to view, however, and he called for a length of fabric for draping the front of the structure. Bolts of it were on hand to be cut into the pieces used to mount sets of buttons.

Ebenezer was immensely pleased with this temporary arrangement and decided at once to make standing work his usual practice. It would save time to eliminate the transition from sitting to standing, and he would hold a commanding position within his office if he were already at his full height when visitors entered—all the more so with those who had never seen such a desk. They would be taken by surprise.

By jove, he realized, he could do the idea one better. What flashed into his mind was a church pulpit at elevation, and he summoned his workmen for two changes: The standing desk would rest upon a platform, and its top would have low walls at the front and sides to keep his work out of view and conceal that much more of him. Presiding behind such an edifice, he would be a man of mystery on high. All the better to work his will on everyone he encountered.

He became so absorbed in this invention that his planned time of departure passed without his realizing it. *Wait until Belle sees this*—that was the thought that made him realize that he was running late.

Blanching, he bolted out of the factory to the street and bellowed for a carriage. The prior day, he had walked to Classic Buttons, but now there was no time for that.

By good fortune, a cab pulled up almost immediately. By ill fortune, its wheels threw spray from a puddle onto Ebenezer's trouser cuffs and shoes. Aggh! But there was no time to think about it. Ebenezer leapt in, called out the address and implored the driver to hurry.

"Have you a rag, by chance?" he asked.

The driver put the reins in one hand, reached down

near his feet, and produced a cloth.

"A clean rag?" said Ebenezer.

"That is the clean one, guv'nor."

"I'll pass, thank you."

"Sorry, sir."

Ebenezer made do by turning his gloves inside out and dabbing at the splash. He gingerly reversed the gloves and put them back on, grimacing at the damp grime within. Just then a gust of wind blew off his hat.

"Stop! Stop!" he cried.

The driver slowed. Ebenezer tossed coins at him for the fare, leapt out and ran back for his hat, howling as it fell under the wheel of a passing cart.

He snatched it up glowering at the crease. No time to think about it. He jammed it on and raced up the street and across, dodging traffic.

In his haste he tripped and took a hard scraping. Leaping up, he found both knees of his trousers scuffed. One had a tiny tear.

He stifled the roar that rose within him. The grime, the damage, the delay! Now, of all times! But there was nothing to be done. He could only shake his head and try to clap stains from himself. After all of his expense and care, this is how he must stand before Belle, and presumably Archie as well. It was already past the time that he had promised to appear.

He straightened, drew a breath, smoothed his expression, marched the final few steps and made a quick rap on the shop door before opening it and entering.

forty

Humiliating arrival

Belle and Archie were standing, Belle a few steps closer to the door.

Yet again, Ebenezer found beauty in Belle that chased away everything in his mind. She was all there was. He hung in dreamy stasis until he noticed her mouth moving and her glance toward her father.

"I beg your pardon?" he said.

"Good morning, Ebenezer." Her light laugh told him that she was repeating herself.

"Yes! Good morning! And to you, Archie."

"Aye, it is, Ebenezer. We could use a bit more sun, but isn't that the way?" He stepped forward for a handshake.

"It is the way, it is. But it is pleasant and dry outside … save a few puddles." He gestured sheepishly to his various besmirchings. "I deeply regret my appearance and tardiness. My realizing the latter led to the former."

"I'm sorry for your misfortune," said Belle. "Did you run—or perhaps tumble—all the way here?" she teased.

"I certainly did not leave myself enough time. I am mortified."

"I'm just glad you are here, safe and sound."

"Safe, anyway."

"I was going to suggest another short walk," said Belle, "but if you have found this a dodgy morning to go out of doors—"

"Not at all. I would be delighted. Surely no worse can befall me today." Awkwardness bloomed here, given the prior day's question, yet unanswered.

"Manure," said Archie.

Ebenezer swallowed.

" —would be worse," Archie continued, "to have

befall you, I mean. That's what you need to watch out for."

"Father!"

"Terrible to step in."

"Indeed it is," said Ebenezer.

This provided a chuckle on which to exit.

"We shall return shortly, Father."

"Of course, Dearest. I'll be right here."

forty-one

The answer

Once outside, without conferring about their route, the pair turned up the walk and into the passage between buildings.

"What an oaf I am," said Ebenezer. "To be late and arrive such a mess! Unforgivable. And yet I do beg your forgiveness."

"Granted," said Belle, brightly. "Do let us help you— Father and I—repair your clothing. He trained as a tailor, did you know?"

"No, is that so?"

"Yes, and clothing repairs are a small sideline of ours. We can fix you up as good as new."

"Even my hat?" Ebenezer removed and brandished the same. It was a rueful joke. He knew that it was dented beyond hope.

"Well, almost as good as new," Belle said. "Milliners we are not."

Just then, a rare wash of light filled the air, the sun at such an angle that it reached them even between the buildings.

"Ah, there's the sun," Ebenezer said, raising his hat for shade. Then dropping his gaze and finding Belle's eyes, he said, "No, there it is."

Belle laughed. "Oh, you."

He replaced his hat. "Or the sister of the sun, perhaps. Blinding in radiance."

"I could become accustomed to these remarks."

"I would be happy to oblige."

"And I would be happy to … accept."

They stopped and faced each other.

" —your proposal."

"Yes?"

"Yes."

"Yes?"

"Yes!"

Ebenezer swept Belle into his arms.

"My darling."

"My dearest."

They kissed and then stood back beaming.

"Darling Belle," said Ebenezer, "I shall endeavor to— "

But Belle cut him off with a light touch on his arm and a nod of her head toward the far end of the alley.

There, standing and staring, was the very same elderly woman from the previous day. Ebenezer doffed his misshapen top hat with one hand, then added the other hand and repeated his shooing motion from the previous encounter. With a glare and the same huff that she had made before, the woman continued on her way.

Belle and Ebenezer laughed holding onto each other. Then they kissed again.

forty-two

A father waits

Back in the shop, Archie was not working. He had not the capacity. At a time like this, who gave a button about buttons?

"My little Blue Bell," he sighed.

"Our little Blue Bell," he corrected for the sake of Lily. He did not share Belle's ability to commune with his late beloved, but he did speak to her frequently and listen for her replies.

"She loves him, Lil, as you can see, and I like him very much. He is a strong young man. Strong in mind, strong in spirit. A little odd perhaps, with an unusual intensity. But you know, he reminds me of you in that way! Not his oddity, his intensity. Who knows, maybe he will be able to speak to you as well. Belle could make an introduction. 'Mother, this is Ebenezer. Ebenezer, this is … your mother-in-law, Lily.'" At this imagining, he slumped and wiped his eyes with his handkerchief.

"I miss you, my love. I despise that you are not here. For you not to share times like these—it's just not right. Not right."

His gaze lingered on the shop door. "They will come in any moment now, and I will rise. Belle will come to me for a hug, then she will step to the side. Ebenezer's hat— his poor mashed hat—will be in his hand. That hat! Those sorry knees! Did you see? I fear he took a tumble just before coming in the d— "

"Oh, my," Archie murmured. "Oh my. You didn't! Did you? Did you trip him, Lily Cross Endicott?

forty-three

Memories

Recollection had flooded back. He, Archie, had suffered the very same misfortune as Ebenezer, finding himself a mess at the crucial moment of asking his beloved's hand. Except his clumsiness came directly in view of Lily's father, old Tristram Cross.

Archie had been the poorest of church mice back then, apprenticed to a tailor for nearly four years. He and Lily had been schoolmates. She originally had paid him no mind, hang as he might at the edge of her circle. Finally, one day when they were teens—and she from birth a sassy lass—Lily plunked down beside him at a to-do on the green and took a sip of his pint. She immediately spit it out, choking until he had to thump her back. The loveliest of backs. She laughed as she became able to breathe again. Her sparkling eyes found his, and she fell quiet, seeing something in them for the first time.

The very next day Archie began an extended act of hopeful affirmation. He arranged with his master, Charles Rabold, to keep a bolt of second-quality cloth so that he might fashion himself a suit. This became a key part of his education. He worked on it little by little for months, using it to faster gain a hand for tailoring. But a few months in, Rabold stopped him.

"You have made the worst of your mistakes and have become quite skillful," said Rabold. "Now you must start again with better cloth."

"Why, sir?"

"I have seen you with that girl, that Lily Cross."

"Oh?"

"Yes, oh. And I know what you are doing."

"You do?"

"You are making your wedding suit."

"Am I?"

Rabold glared at him.

"I am," admitted Archie.

"Yes, and it must have better cloth."

He started again.

forty-four

A chaotic proposal

And what a suit Archie made. His masterpiece. It made him look and feel taller. He could hardly feel smaller, so short and slight was he, but the suit gave him power. He took care never to let Lily see it. Not until he arrived at her home by prearrangement, for them to spend time together on his birthday. He knocked on the door, and Lily swung it aside.

"Oh, Arch, look at you!"

"Look at you." He offered her a small clutch of flowers.

"Oh, thank you! But you should not be the one giving gifts! Happy birthday!" She hugged him.

"Thank you," he said mid-embrace. "I do have hopes for a particular present."

"Oh?" Lily said, drawing back. Then she realized what he meant. "Oh!"

She placed one hand on his chest to nudge him backward and shut the door behind her. Their eyes locked.

"You, Lil. You are the gift I want forever."

"Archie," she said softly.

"Will you be my wife?"

"Yes. Will you be my husband?"

"Yes."

Archie leaned forward, and Lily met him in a kiss. They leaned back to look at each other.

"I will do my utmost to honor and care for you, my darling," Archie said.

"And I you."

They beamed.

"Is your father at home?"

"Working in the shed." Lily motioned toward the outbuilding behind Archie.

"I'll go now," he said. "Wish me luck."

Lily hauled him in for another kiss, then spun him about. He drew in a breath, stepped forward … and promptly went sprawling.

"Loafer!" cried Lily.

A series of barks followed. Archie had tripped over a dog.

"Bad dog, Loafer! Oh, Archie, your beautiful suit!"

Chagrined, Archie stood and inspected his clothing, finding a patch of grit on each knee and a swath of it on his left shoulder.

"Oh bother! Let me get a brush for you!" said Belle, dashing into the house, calling again, "Bad Loafer!"

Delicately, Archie used his gloved fingers to remove what particles he could. Attending to this contributed to his failing to hear an oncoming rush until he was again knocked from his feet. It was another dog.

"Squiz!"

The hound was squirming on top of Archie licking his face.

"Squiz!" This second bellow was mingled with laughter. Both cries had come from Lily's father, Tristram Cross, a harness maker.

"Stop that now!" Cross ordered. He hurried forward and shooed away the dog.

"Beg pardon, Archie," he said. He dropped a hand toward the young man, who took it and found himself quickly hauled up.

"Let's look at you now," Cross said, putting his hand to Archie's elbow to turn him about. "Why, what a fine suit you have!"

"Thank you, sir." Archie turned to face him, even as he discreetly reached behind himself to sweep pebbles from the seat of his pants.

"Squiz! You didn't!" This was Lily, returning from the house.

"He did, I'm afraid," her father said. "Knocked Archie on his arse."

"Father!"

"Terribly sorry, young man."

"Quite all right," said Archie.

"It's not all right!" said Lily, busy with the brush that she had retrieved. "You in your new suit! Why would you want to join all this hubbub?" She clapped a hand over her blurting.

"New suit?" Cross said. "Join this hubbub?"

Lily mouthed an apology to Archie, who shook it off with an assuring if nervous grin.

"Archie, you sharp devil," said Cross. "Have something to ask me, young man?"

"I do, sir." He cleared his throat. "Lily and I would like to marry. With your blessing and that of Mrs. Cross."

Lily slipped her hand into his, and they stood facing her father. He regarded the pair for a moment, then laid his hands on their outside shoulders.

"Ardelia!" Cross bellowed over their heads toward the house. "We'd like to see you out here, please! There's news!"

Mrs. Cross emerged amid much additional barking of the dogs. She was as pleased as her husband and hugged the freshly-engaged couple as Loafer and Squiz chased each other around them all.

"Welcome to this mess, my boy!" said Cross. "We're glad to have you."

"Glad to join, sir."

Thankfully, Archie's suit bore no lasting damage. He looked grand at their wedding. Sadly, only fourteen years later, he wore it to Lily's funeral.

Chuckling at the recollection, eyes brimming, Archie spoke in a soft theatrical imitation of old Tristram Cross, who had dearly loved to hold little Belle. "Lily! We'd like to see you here, please! There's news!"

He said this as he peered out the window and saw Belle and Ebenezer returning, holding hands and smiling.

forty-five

A knowledge gap

They agreed to defer their wedding. At the very least, Ebenezer wished to wait until the end of the year, to solidify matters in his fledgling business. Belle preferred a spring wedding, so that meant several more months.

"And perhaps not next year?" suggested Ebenezer.

"The following spring?" said Belle.

"Would you mind terribly?"

"Honestly, I would not. It is all so new and unusual— and delightful!—simply to be engaged. I would rather not rush through it."

"I feel just the same. We've spent our entire lives not

being engaged, and all of our days hence will be married. Does it not seem wise to devote ample time to this in-between state?"

"It does. I am so glad we agree."

And so they, quite literally, went about business as before, with the exception of being promised to each other. They became adept at shifting between modes— employer and employee when discussing buttons and button-making, future husband and wife at all other times.

Each month, they playfully acknowledged the return of their engagement date, wishing each other a happy anniversary.

The third such time, Ebenezer said, "I have a proposal."

"You have made it," joked Belle. "That is what we are memorializing."

"This is a different but related proposal."

"Oh?"

"A change in reference to our monthly anniversary."

"What change, sir, do you suggest?"

"A shift to the correct term. An anniversary is a yearly remembrance. The word comes from the Latin *annus*. So a monthly anniversary doesn't make sense, does it?"

"Indeed not. So a monthly remembrance would be … ?"

"A mensiversary."

Belle made a small smile. "I respectfully decline that proposal, Dearest."

Ebenezer was taken aback. "But it is from the Latin for month, *mensis*."

"Yes, and *menses* is already taken."

"Already taken?"

"By another monthly occurrence, of course."

"It is? What do you mean?"

"Do you not know?"

"I do not. Is it a matter between you and your father?"

"No, no, no." Belle was chuckling now.

"Your mother, then? It cannot refer to our weekly visits to her grave." Ebenezer said "our" because he had come to participate in these memorials.

"It certainly has more to do with Mother than with Father, but— "

"I'm sorry, but I'm utterly confounded, Dear. What don't I know?"

"This is rather a delicate matter, Ben." This had become her pet name for Ebenezer. At first it gave him pause, but he had come to quite like the sound of "Ben and Belle.") "But as wife and husband, we will share all manner of intimacies, so ... " Ebenezer looked away decorously here, but with a light grin.

"'Menses' has a particular meaning for women." Belle searched Ebenezer's eyes but still found no recognition.

"What is it?"

"This is the rare gap in your vast knowledge, my dear. Brace yourself." She leaned in and murmured further explanation. The face of her fiancé flushed.

"Now you know, sir," Belle said, patting his chest.

"This is true?"

"Sadly but remarkably so. You will even find it in the Bible."

"Where?"

"Many places. It is called an issue of blood."

"Is that what that means?"

"Yes, Ben."

He sat back to marvel.

"May I ask how you ... that is, how do women ... ?"

"... address this issue?"

She leaned in again and told more. He leaned back

and looked at her with further marveling. She nodded that yes, it was true.

His thoughts reeled to the women in his shop. He had given no consideration to the matter of bodily waste from his employees beyond providing the usual outdoor privy. Yet, unfathomably, this was an additional stream of waste of which he had been completely unaware.

"I had no idea," he breathed.

"So I see."

"It makes me wonder what else I do not know. Or have not perceived."

"We will be of great help to each other in this way. Broadening our perspectives."

"Exactly. In that regard, may I ask you a favor?"

"Anything, Dearest."

"Would you visit the factory and give me your thoughts?"

"Ah! Happily, yes!"

"And speak to some of the women there? Discreetly inquire about whatever you see fit?"

"It would be my honor and joy."

And so she did.

forty-six

A factory visit and then ...

Ebenezer took great pride in showing Belle the entire facility—from the loud machines to the carefully-labeled storage system to the chaotic repair shop tables.

Many of the male employees tried and failed to feign disinterest in the boss's comely fiancée. Others did not bother disguising their curiosity. Some of the female employees seemed to regard Belle with disdain, but Ebenezer saw many of these thaw at her warm smile, respectful questions and careful listening. A few threw a cautious glance toward Ebenezer, and Belle gestured for him to withdraw. After busying himself elsewhere and finding Belle's eye from across the manufacturing floor, she motioned for him to turn about and keep minding his own business. He raised his eyebrows but did so, noting in the process sly smiles from some of the workers looking on. Belle took her time in the building and met or at least nodded a greeting to every last one of his employees.

After Belle's tour concluded, Ebenezer invited her to enjoy the view from behind his unique standing desk.

"Do you really hide behind this all day?" she said.

"It is not hiding, and I spend much of my time out on the work floor, but in all other respects, you are exactly correct."

"Do you stand here and think of me?"

"At times."

"At times?"

"I think of you all the day."

"This is a good place to hide."

"Better than many."

"Better than all the desks."

"Better than—bless us!—every one."

They left the factory in high spirits and strolled for miles through the city, falling into sober discussion around Belle's observations about the working conditions.

"It is chilly throughout the building," she said.

"Of course it is, at this time of year. The entire building can't be warm."

"Can it not?"

"Impossible."

"It cannot be impossible."

"Why not?"

"Much larger buildings are heated: Cathedrals, courts, prisons. How is that done?"

"With money."

"They burn money?"

"Or they have it to burn. They use expensive systems: Steam heat, coal furnaces. Not only expensive to install, but expensive to run, due to repeated purchases of wood or coal or both."

"I see."

"As well as labor to handle the wood and coal, and that costs more yet. Out of the question."

"Leaving your workers to suffer from the cold."

"As do I. My office has no heat, and I spend much time out on the floor. During winter we are all cold."

"But at least you get to move about. Many of the workers stay in one position all day."

"As they would in other occupations. Many workers are out of doors all day with no walls to protect them. Peddlers, street sweepers— "

"But they move about, Ben, and that does something to help them stay warm. And some can duck into shops or hospitals or stables—places of the sort—to at least briefly get warm."

"The factory does have a stove. The employees have interludes to warm themselves."

"And pauses to use the privy, but everyone at the same time, so there are uncomfortable waits, and there is only one privy and only one stove."

"I have not heard complaints. The conditions are no worse than at other factories, and better than many."

"Are you willing to hear complaints?"

"Naturally I am willing, though many I will not be able to heed."

"Would you receive a complaint from Laurie, the youngest of your button-makers, as readily as you hear my thoughts on this? Or Rose, the eldest of the women? Or Charlotte? Or Abigail? Or— "

"Certainly, I would listen to any of them."

"And a complaint from any of your male employees? Philip? Charley? Dear old Michael?"

"Of course."

"Then consider yourself to be hearing a complaint. I spoke to those women and men and many more and over and over they mentioned the cold. Mind me, you must not lay the grievance on any name that I have mentioned. They might or might not have said anything at all. I was only trying to make the matter more personal for you. They represent all of the employees. Your workers are freezing, Ben, and it is not enough to say that they would freeze elsewhere, too. You must aim to do better."

"Well, I— "

"Just as you did with your desk."

"I thought you liked my desk."

"I love your desk."

"But now you make it sound selfish."

"It's not selfish, it's practical. And this is also a practical matter. If your workers were not struggling to stay warm, they would have more energy to put toward making buttons. Does your production slow down when it is cold?"

"It does. I consider that a natural development."

"It is, but elsewhere you battle nature. The walls of your factory combat nature. Buttons themselves—your very products—are weapons against nature, because they fasten clothing. Bowing to nature is no excuse. It's not what you do at other times, and it is not worthy of you.

It's just being miserly."

"Miserly!"

"Miserly! Your workers are miserable, and it is your doing."

"Come, my dear. You exaggerate."

"I am not exaggerating. They are suffering for long hours."

"I cannot change the entire world for every person."

"You can change a corner of it for a few people. For your people."

"What corner?"

"Find a corner, literally, to add another stove. Find a spot to add another privy."

"You do not understand the costs, Dear Belle."

"Do not 'Dear Belle' me about this, Ben. I understand costs. I know you have to make a profit. But there are human costs as well, and there are humane investments that will return profit. Your workers will stay with you longer if you put something toward their comfort. You will not have to train as many replacements."

Ebenezer fell silent, his mouth a tight line. Belle lightly touched his sleeve.

"Are you not the giant who will straddle London, Mr. Scrooge? This is not too big for you to do. You have eyes to see what is needed and the power to do something about it. Lend your might to those who are weaker. It does not suit you, sir, to be only as good as anyone else. Aim to be better."

"Better than every one?" Ebenezer said, lightly echoing their earlier exchange.

"Better than, bless us, every one!"

They stopped, kissed, and turned toward Belle's home, suspending all talk of business. Soon they were laughing.

Once inside the shop door, however, their gaiety fell away at once. Because they found Archie on the floor on his back unmoving.

Belle flew to him with a cry, Ebenezer just behind.

III

forty-seven

A confusing collapse

Archie stirred. He was pale but breathing. His eyes were closed.

"Father? Father?"

Belle's trembling hands moved about Archie, seeking information. Her eyes widened as she pressed lightly at the base of his throat.

"His heart beat is so slow," she whispered to Ebenezer, who was removing his own coat. He folded it for padding beneath Archie's head. As she slipped this into place, Belle gently felt about her father's skull. "No swelling," she said.

Archie's eyes fluttered open, his expression befuddled.

"I'm here, Father, I'm here."

Archie looked a question at her, then moved his eyes about, searching. "Just lie still," said Belle.

Archie's lips moved, but he produced no sound. "Wha— ?" he finally managed. "Wha— ?"

"Shhh," said Belle. "Can you understand me?" Archie gave a slight nod.

"We found you on the floor."

"Lily?" Archie said. "You and Lily ... found me?"

"Ebenezer and I."

"Ebbuh … nee … "

He leaned in with a reassuring smile.

"Hello, Archie."

"Beezer," said Archie vaguely.

His eyes returned to his daughter. "Blue Bell," he said.

"Yes, Father."

"Lily?"

"Just close your eyes for now, Father."

Archie complied and let himself relax. Belle turned to Ebenezer, her face tight with distress.

forty-eight

Uncertainty

Soon Archie opened his eyes, and Belle saw comprehension. He squeezed her hand.

"Did I fall?" he said.

"We don't know, Father. We just returned from a walk."

"I don't remember falling. The last thing I knew, I was working … but now I'm here."

"You were as pale as ivory, Father. Your color is better now." She felt his throat again. "Your heart beat is stronger. It was terribly slow. Do you feel able to sit up?"

"I could try."

Ebenezer leaned in to offer his hand.

"Ah, Ebenezer," said Archie. "There you are." He took the hand. "Thank you."

"Don't stand" said Belle, "just try sitting up." With

their help, Archie carefully sat and shook his head to clear it.

"I'm fine now," he said.

"Are you?" said Belle.

He nodded, and they helped him stand. He took care to hold the edge of the counter.

"All better," Archie proclaimed with a weak smile. But again he shook his head. "I wonder what happened?" They all wondered.

Belle suggested that Archie lie down for a bit, and he agreed. While Belle helped her father to his bed, Ebenezer retrieved his coat and set about straightening and smoothing it. After Belle returned, she went to him for an embrace.

"What is the matter with him, Ben? I'm afraid."

"I wish I knew. Has anything like that happened before?"

"Never."

"He didn't hit his head when he fell?"

"I don't think so. There's still no swelling. I felt the back of his head again as he laid back on his pillow."

"That is fortunate."

"Yes, but he could fall again."

"Perhaps he felt it coming on—his collapse—and somehow eased himself down."

"But what is it that came on?"

"A touch of fever?"

"He was cool to the touch, though."

"So pale, at first."

"Yes! Then his skin was cooler yet. I would even say clammy."

"So he somehow lost blood to his head? I suppose all of us feel light-headed when we stand too quickly."

"But not enough to faint away. A fragile maiden, perhaps, but not Father."

"Did he say anything more about your mother?"

"No. That broke my heart. He truly was looking about for her, don't you think?"

"Absolutely."

"So confused."

"I'm confused as well, by all of this."

Belle sighed heavily and pressed closer to Ebenezer.

forty-nine

Questions deepen

They continued speaking softly and were conducting some minor tidying when Archie emerged into the shop not a quarter of an hour later. One hand on the back of his neck, he stretched and grimaced.

"Well, this isn't like me," he said.

Belle and Ebenezer hurried to his side. Archie put his arms around Belle and reached for Ebenezer's hand even as she was squeezing him tight.

"Napping away the afternoon!" he said. "I'm not even sure when I lay down."

"It was only a few minutes ago, Father."

"Was it?"

"Yes, I only just left you there."

"Left me there?"

Belle looked to Ebenezer and then back at Archie.

"What is the last thing you remember, Father?"

"Why, bidding you farewell on your walk. And then working. I must have grown sleepy and decided to lie down for a few winks. But you say you left me there?"

"Yes, Father."

They gently explained discovering him and walked him through the details.

"I remember none of that. Not a bit. You are quite sure?"

"Certain, Father."

Archie's face was drawn. "Perhaps I should lie down again."

And he did. Somewhat later, he emerged with fresh confusion, and Belle had to share the same explanation again.

fifty

Ongoing mystery

Thus began a new pattern in their lives. Archie was able to work as well as ever, but his memory was ridiculously faulty. There was no change in his remembering ongoing details within the shop, or a daily visitor such as Ebenezer, but he lost his hold on matters that arose less often. He started to forget the names of people who he and Belle knew mainly through their church and thus saw only weekly. He was at a loss with long-time friends whose paths rarely crossed his, and even some relatives who he scarcely saw.

His memory of his youth seemed largely intact, but recent years drained away. He proved to have no recollection of particular trips or incidents during much of Belle's life. For example, he had no recall of the dog Muggins, mentioned earlier, when he came up one day in conversation.

"Your mother fed him, you say?"

"Yes, Father. He was oddly fond of carrots."

"Carrots!"

"Yes. When we could spare a carrot, it went to him. He ate them so quickly that we took care to cut them into small pieces so he wouldn't choke."

"Carrots to a mastiff … " Archie marveled at this, and shook his head at this latest gap in his past.

He continued to collapse from time to time. This happened without warning. He could be working away with full energy, then Belle would look over and find him tipping from his seat or already sprawled on the floor. Miraculously, he managed to escape head injuries during each incident. He learned to take particular care after sitting for long stretches, making sure to hold onto furniture when he rose, and he came to avoid sudden changes in direction, which sometimes seemed to cause his losses of consciousness. But on many occasions when he forgot himself and rose straight from his chair or took a step and pivoted, he was perfectly fine. His blackouts were utterly unpredictable.

Something else developed—a tendency toward brief vacancies. During these incidents, Archie would not collapse or slump or even close his eyes but simply become immobile with an unfocused stare, ceasing to respond. He and Belle might be in merry conversation, tossing remarks back and forth, when Archie would suddenly fall silent. Belle could stand before him and speak his name and wave her hands before his eyes, but he would remain unblinking and stationary save for a slight working of his jaw. In moments, he would emerge befogged, as if awaking from a reverie, and Belle would ask lightly where he had gone.

"Oh, did I go again?"

"Yes, Father. I'm glad to have you back."

He would soon resume conversation. Within half an

hour, he would have no memory of the incident. Belle found that it left a gap in his memory of about twenty minutes, because later in the day he would remember the entire morning and afternoon except for the time surrounding his vacancy. This became clear one day when the two of them happened to see out of their window a bucket of paint fall from a passing cart. It exploded into a spray of color on the street.

"At least it's brown," said Archie at the time. "It'll blend in."

But later the same day, after a vacancy came upon him, Archie saw something through the window and called Belle over.

"Look at that, now. A bucket of paint must have taken a tumble."

"Oh my," said Belle, as if seeing this for the first time. She had learned to simply join Archie in his re-discoveries.

"At least it's brown. It'll blend in."

"Yes, indeed. A happy accident."

Ebenezer offered to pay for a doctor visit, but Belle preferred to wait and remain watchful. As was the case with many of their friends and neighbors, the Endicotts could hardly conceive of visiting a doctor when ailments were not acute, instead relying on close monitoring and a long tradition of home remedies.

"I don't consider Father to be in immediate danger," said Belle to Ebenezer one afternoon when Archie was napping.

"Not from falls?"

"I do worry about that, but I'd be concerned regardless of a doctor's treatment. Even if there is any medicine for such a condition, surely it is not foolproof. I would need to remain as watchful as ever."

"What about his heart?"

"I feel much the same. It seems as strong as ever, save for those moments when he goes pale during one of his collapses. Father has made it clear to me that he would not take any medicine that his heart almost never needs —if there even is a suitable medicine." She imitated his voice: "I will not live out days and weeks in fear of a few moments a month."

"Hm," said Ebenezer.

"What do you think?"

"I don't know what to think. It's his choice, of course."

"I have to tell you something else."

"Yes?"

"That, in a way, he welcomes this."

"Welcomes it!"

"Welcomes them, I might say. His new conditions."

"But why would he ever?"

"He has had the sweetest conversations with me. Heartbreaking but sweet." She proceeded to condense a number of talks for Ebenezer as she relived them.

fifty-one

A solemn exchange

"I never expected to live forever, Blue Bell."

"Oh, Father."

"And I can't say that I don't look forward to seeing your mother. Why should you be the only one who gets to spend time with her?"

"Father— "

"Think of it, Dearest. The day will come when you will take your trips within your spirit and see the two of us, together."

"Father, please, don't." Belle drew him into a tight embrace.

"I can't stay on and on, you know," Archie said over her shoulder.

"Yes, you can, and you will."

"You don't need me anyway."

"How can you say that?" Belle drew back to look at him.

"You are grown now, Darling. You are more able than I ever was. Smarter, quicker ..."

"Father, you overestimate me."

"You underestimate yourself if you don't see it. You are like your mother—strong and sure. Lily was not just my better half, she was half-again my better, and no one can tell me otherwise."

"But— "

"No, child. I am a limited man. I always was. All I can do—could do, in my day—was work hard. I would have foundered without your mother. She was the brains, the sense, the vision. Thank the Lord she passed it on, so I have you to help me. You have all of her, and I could not be happier. You have taken care of me, and I rest easy knowing that you will always be able to take care of yourself."

"Father, you are making me weep."

"And you have Ebenezer now, sweetheart." He nudged her engagement ring. "You will take care of each other, just as Lily and I did. And Lord willing, you will have children to care for, just as your mother and I had you. Our greatest blessing."

"Well, there, then—that's a reason to linger," Belle managed to say, her voice cracking. "To meet your grandchildren. That decides it. You are not allowed to leave."

Archie raised a gentle hand to her cheek, and she pressed against it. "Hear that, head and heart?" Archie said, theatrically clapping his free hand to his skull and then to his chest. "You have your orders."

"You are not allowed to fail," Belle sternly addressed Archie's interior troops. "Keep my papa strong. It is not his time."

"Said with authority."

"It is not your time, Father. Remember that. Remember that."

"You know I won't."

Belle laughed and cried as she finished her story here for Ebenezer.

fifty-two

A voice

The days went by. Weeks. Months. Between work and beginning to blend their lives around Archie and planning their wedding and their future, Belle and Ebenezer were occupied every moment. They discussed having a home that would offer space for button work as well as a spare room for Archie, and they visited some possibilities.

Ebenezer consulted with any doctor who happened into his orbit. Two of these, several weeks apart, kindly swung around to Archie's shop to examine him, and they listened closely to descriptions of his symptoms. In the end, they could do little more than shake their heads. There was nothing to be done.

Ebenezer came to have his own little table at Classic

Buttons, where he could continue his work in the evening, reviewing figures and making notes, so as to be on hand to watch over Archie when Belle made visits to Lily.

"It's kind of you, son," said Archie.

"It's kind of you to let me work here, Father. It's quite cozy."

"And you get all the more time to gaze at Belle."

"There is that." When Belle visited Lily, Ebenezer did treasure the opportunity to feast his eyes on his beloved with no concern of embarrassment. His mind would settle into a calm, drifting state.

Something odd happened one of the times he was so engaged.

Ebbie.

Ebenezer's head snapped up.

"Fan?"

He'd heard the voice of his sister, Fan. Impossible.

Ebbie.

He looked about, then hurried to the shop door to peer up and down the street. No one was there but the usual passers-by. He had not actually expected to find Fan, because something was off about the voice. It was coming from elsewhere, not from his surroundings. If anywhere, it was inside his head. But it was as clear as if his sister were in the room.

"What is it?" Archie inquired.

Ebenezer looked at Belle, still working away in a reverie. She gave no indication of hearing the voice nor of any disturbance to her visit. *Wherever she has traveled,* Ebenezer thought, *Fan is not there.* Which was good. If Belle had heard Fan, that would have put Fan in the proximity of the dead, would it not? His heart clenched at the very thought.

"Ebenezer?" Archie asked. "Are you all right? What

did you hear?"

Ebbie.

"I, er— I thought I heard a voice outside, one I knew —know."

"Oh? I didn't hear a thing. May I ask who?"

"My sister, actually."

"Your sister! How delightful! Do bring her in."

"If she's out there, but I don't see her. I'll just step out to— " Then he thought better of it, pausing as he started through the door.

Archie waved him on. "Go, go. I'll be fine."

"Just for a bit," promised Ebenezer, hurrying out.

He moved quickly, looking in all directions, hungry to see Fan. He knew that it made no sense and that he would not find her. If Fan were in the area, she would not have walked by the shop. He had given her the address when he had written her about his engagement. And this disembodied repetition of her pet name for him—it was not natural.

He was agitated now. The voice had shaken him from his transfixed watching of Belle, startling him like a sudden hand on the shoulder. It made him think that he had begun to enter that ethereal realm. Had he been about to join Belle on her latest mysterious voyage?

Bah. He shook his head at the thought. He did not want to meet Belle's mother.

There, he had finally admitted it to himself. He was bitter toward the ghost who usurped his fiancée's time.

He had gradually realized this. His fascination with Belle's journeys had given way to resentment. It was not only that Belle took her leave without him, but that she returned refreshed and renewed. It irked him that someone other than he affected her so. Lily was a rival.

Ebenezer disliked his own thoughts in this vein, but they persisted. He found himself brooding in his bed at night. Lily might have taken up Belle's time if she were alive, of course, but it bothered him that death had no effect. When Archie died—as much as Ebenezer genuinely liked him—he could only expect the same. Lily would always have a separate life that he could never know.

He had gained an absurd preoccupation: Why cannot the dead be gone forever?

Especially you, he found himself thinking. The thought was aimed at his father. He despised the idea of seeing him again.

He often struck his temple as the maddening notions piled up. If it so happened that he could do what Belle did—see Lily—then might he not also encounter his late father, Percival? Ebenezer had been so at odds with Percival that his heart had leapt at hearing of his death. Yet it brought bitterness as well. He did not understand his own reaction. Logic suggested that if he had truly wanted to be rid of his father, losing him would have brought only calm. Why did this scalding feeling remain?

To his dismay, his rage spilled over to Fan. With just the right blend of mettle and sweetness, she had managed to remain close to their father, and she had never stopped trying to draw him and Ebenezer together. She wrote long letters on the subject that were marvels of decency and diplomacy, acknowledging Ebenezer's reasons for animosity while also urging him to visit and attempt yet another reconciliation while there was time. He resisted these entreaties even as Percival became ill and weak. Ultimately the point was moot—Percival passed away. Fan had written shattering lines to him about this:

> *I do hope this will be a comfort for you to hear, Dearest Ebbie—Father reached out to you at the end. He said to tell you that he understood why you had not come, that*

135

*he would have done the same in your place. He took all
the blame for the chasm between you and he. His exact
words were: "Tell Ebenezer not to worry. Tell him I am
proud of him, of his success. Tell him I know that he is a
tremendous businessman whom none will approach.
Tell him that I know he will make the name Scrooge
shine forever."*

Frenzied at this recollection, Ebenezer swung into
the space between buildings where he had proposed to
Belle. The Joyful Passage, they had playfully come to call
it. But here alone, without his beloved, it appeared to him
only a dismal alley. He reflexively reached toward a wall
to confirm his new perception but paused before making
contact with the dingy stone. On the facing building was
was dirty, rotting wood. Why had he never seen this? He
stood in the middle of "The Joyful Passage" and clenched
his fists, then stretched his face to the sky and dragged in
quick breaths through his nose.

"Calm yourself," he admonished. "Calm yourself."

Then: *Enough.* He must go back to Archie.

When he returned, *Ah no!* Belle was kneeling beside
her father, stretched out on the floor.

fifty-three

After the fall

"Father? Father!" Belle's voice was frantic.

Ebenezer flew to her side as her hands skimmed
Archie's skull.

"Did he hit his head?"

"I don't know. He was like this when I returned. I don't know for how long."

"It wasn't long. I was only outside for a moment. I'm sorry, but I thought I heard— "

"Father?" Archie was stirring now. He opened his eyes. "Father?"

His eyes bright, Archie patted Belle's hand. "Lil," he said. "My darling Lil. Look at you. Just look at you." He stared straight into Belle's eyes.

"Archie," Belle whispered, even as her eyes brimmed with tears.

The wonder in Archie's face was like sunrise.

"Belle," he said.

"Yes?"

" —has become such a marvelous woman, Dearest. So smart, so strong. My heart bursts just to look at her. But of course, you know. You talk to her."

"I do."

"She'll be just fine without me."

"Will she?"

"Oh, yes, yes, not a doubt. She can run the shop better than I ever could. Or do anything she likes. She is a full partner to Ebenezer. Ben, she calls him. Such a good lad. So good for Belle. And she for him. You have seen."

"Yes, I have."

"Belle and Ben. I will miss them."

"You do not have to," whispered Belle.

"Oh, you. It's all right. We'll watch over them together. I will say goodbye and come to see you soon."

"Take your time."

"Soon."

Archie closed his eyes and relaxed into stillness.

For the first time, there was indeed a bit of swelling toward the back of his skull. They had discussed what they would do in such a case. Ebenezer seized a fabric bag and some oilcloth that they had set aside, hurried to an ice man and brought back ice. They wrapped it in sacking and kept it pressed to the swelling.

As it became clear that Archie would remain unconscious, Belle and Ebenezer carefully maneuvered him onto a blanket and then, each taking an end of it, they conveyed him to his bed. Belle lovingly smoothed his hair. Ebenezer placed his hands on her shoulders, and Belle reached up to cover one of them with her own hand. In time, they slipped from the room.

"I'm sorry I left him," said Ebenezer.

Belle shook her head. "Don't be. It could as well have been me. It has been."

"But not with such injury."

"No, there is no blame," Belle said firmly. "You have saved him again and again. Saved us. Given us … more time." Her voice broke on the final words.

Ebenezer took her hand. Belle looked into his eyes.

"What would we have done without you?"

fifty-four

A new idea

After that, Archie was never the same.

"I've started to find him sitting at his work but not working," Belle told Ebenezer as they talked in the front room during yet another of Archie's naps. "Just looking off, but not in one of his vacancies, because he responds if I speak to him."

"Lost in thought, then?"

"Or in not thinking. It's a different type of vacancy. I

see little sign of anything happening in his mind. He sits there like a mannequin, and then might drop into a nap. It can be hours of ... nothing."

Ebenezer nodded, remained still for a time, then shifted uncomfortably. Belle had become adept at intuiting his state of mind, and she responded.

"I know what that movement means."

"Do you?"

"Yes, that is your switching to businessman, and you are exactly right to do so." She altered her posture as well and said, "Speak to Classic Buttons about this situation."

"Yes, I'd like to." He straightened, and his manner subtly stiffened.

"Is it correct to say that Classic Buttons can no longer produce buttons?"

Belle swallowed and spoke softly. "Effectively, yes. Father goes in and out of alertness and productivity, and the most I can hope is that he'll be able to finish out the current orders. But I honestly cannot expect even that. When he is clear in mind, I will tell him that we need to go to the customers to express our regret."

Ebenezer nodded.

"Of course I can still sew. But even that presents a challenge, because I am at my most efficient when I sew as if— " She faltered here " —as if I were alone. But now I must divide my attention between Father and my work, and— "

She paused but managed to continue. "You are kind to listen, Mr. Scrooge"—without irony, this is how she addressed him when they discussed business—"but I am dithering. Father and I must face the truth, as difficult as it might be. Our enterprise of Classic Buttons cannot continue. I say this with sorrow, not only because of what it means for us, but because it means the end of our partnership with you. It is now a commitment that is impossible to keep. You have my fervent and sincere apology."

"Miss Endicott," said Ebenezer, softly addressing her in kind, "I also lament the end of this partnership. Our arrangement was something I never could have foreseen —neither its beginning nor its end after much too short a time. It has been bright and fruitful. I could not be more grateful that I passed through the door of your father's shop and introduced myself. All of my expectations have been surpassed. I see in it the hand of providence. Sadly, in these recent days I also see the hand of misfortune, and you have my deepest sympathy."

"What kind words, Mr. Scrooge. Thank you. They say you are a hard man of business, but just now you remind me of my beloved and endlessly-thoughtful friend Ben."

"Oh?" said Ebenezer, allowing a slight smile, but only briefly. "Let me make sure that I am as firm as required. With delicacy, I must say that the loss of Classic Buttons is a blow to my enterprise. I had hoped to continue to differentiate my business in part by being able to offer nostalgic designs. But at least for now, I will simply have to discontinue that effort."

"Might I make a suggestion?"

"By all means."

"I have given this much thought, but I must say that I cannot judge whether there is commercial merit. I am inevitably bound to it emotionally. So I earnestly desire your perspective."

"Most intriguing. Please continue."

"My idea is to write a book."

"Oh? What about?"

"My thought is to capture Father's knowledge of the craft and the trade of button-making before it is too late. As you have helped us understand, this practice and these capabilities will soon be swept into the past." She swallowed here. "That is much to lose. Too much."

"Indeed."

"My hope is not only to create a record but also a means of instruction for anyone who might want to continue the practice, as Classic Buttons has done, within this dizzying new world of modern manufacturing. If you cannot find another shop such as ours, and another willing button-maker such as Father, but you still want to offer these kinds of secondary products, such a book could help teach someone to make them. Even if you did find another button-maker with Father's experience, that person would presumably be near his own age and perhaps in poor health also, and—well, the need is inevitable."

"What a splendid idea, Miss Endicott. You simply must do this."

"Yes?"

"Absolutely, I insist. You will have my full support. It is a wise investment."

"I'm so pleased that it seems so to you. I trust that this project will let me spend time with Father in the shop without my— " she fluttered a hand—"floating away into other worlds. Of course, it will mean that I will need to suspend my sewing. But to care for Father, I would have to anyway."

"And your mother … ?"

"Yes, I have thought endlessly about that. It will mean not seeing her."

"Is that—acceptable?"

"I spoke to her about it."

"Oh?"

"She understands. No, more than that. She helped me toward the thought of the book during my final visit with her."

"Final visit?"

Her eyes welled up.

"Belle, dearest," Ebenezer said, suddenly no longer "Mr. Scrooge."

"Yes, Ben?"

"You are speaking about this rather lightly, I think. Tell me: Is there any possibility that you will no longer visit your mother?"

"There is."

"Oh, Belle."

"Not just a possibility. It is certain." Her mind went to the conversation.

fifty-five

A final parting

Mother, how can we even be discussing this?

How can we not?

Never seeing each other again?

Everything has its season. And our season together has run long. We have had extra time.

Mother. You make it sound unnatural.

It could only be called super-natural: Beyond the natural. Our cup has overflowed and still been filled.

Must it end?

It is a matter of choice.

Are you choosing for it to end?

You are.

I am not! I don't want it to. You brought this up.

You are, my dear, though you might not realize it. And I support the choice. I agree. It is for the best.

Mother! I'm not— How can you say—

Belle. We both see that it must be so. It is good, it is right. To let us go, your father and me.

Father is still here.

He will be with me soon. You know that.

You keep telling me I know things I do not know! I don't!

Lily waited for Belle to quiet.

You do know.

Belle wept.

You will have your own family.

If I do, I will want to talk to you about them, about your grandchildren.

You can, you will. To me and to your father. We will see you and hear you. We simply will not answer directly. That is the way of life and the afterlife.

It has not been the way.

And we can be grateful for that. No one is granted what we have been granted—to commune after life has ended. This is not a loss. It has been only gain.

Mother. Mother. I cannot lose you again.

Only gain. Not loss. Only gain.

Belle collapsed into herself, her heart rending. She could not say how long she wept.

Finally, for what she knew would be the final time, Belle raised her eyes and found her mother beholding her. She opened her mouth to speak, but there was too much to voice.

I know, Belle. I know, I know, I know. You are my baby, my darling, my love. I will always watch over you. Always.

And she was gone.

Belle told Ebenezer this, doubled over into his arms sobbing.

fifty-six

A book develops, but ...

Archie lived for twelve more weeks, almost through the end of the year, as the chill of the season descended. He never made another button. It was a difficult time. Also a fortunate time.

Archie was often uncomfortable, plagued by swimming vision, poor balance, and fatigue. Such fatigue. He complained of poor sleep at night and yet napped often and nodded off mid-conversation. When staying awake, he often rambled unpredictably. Much of it was about Lily. He spoke to her as if she were present, about topics that Belle generally could not decipher.

"This must be put in the post, Lil, but I have to finish this batch. Could you take Belle?" ... "Remember that time in the woods, with the fire?" ... "I came around the corner near the butcher's and saw a woman who took my breath away, and for an instant, I didn't recognize you! I got to see you again for the first time." His face often glowed during these waking dreams, and the sight gave Belle a thrill that would taper to sorrow at her growing sense that Archie's next life was drawing him from this one. She let herself feel joy in that, even as the impending loss squeezed her heart.

She did write the book about button-making. She

decided early in the undertaking that it would bear
Archie's name even if the work was hers. She considered
herself a historian and archivist speaking on his behalf.
She found that she knew a great deal about button-
making from being involved with each stage, if
sometimes only at the edges. She knew virtually
everything about the materials that her father purchased,
and about his suppliers, because for years she had placed
his orders. She knew the workings of the equipment and
all stages of the processes. In the section of the book that
addressed sewing cloth covers onto buttons, she took a
sly pleasure in writing about herself in the third person.
There, for the sake of consistency with the other text, she
had to avoid saying too much, since she could furnish
endless information. Her eyes brimmed when she
sketched how young Belle learned her trade from her
mother Lily, who had been taken from the shop and from
their home much too soon.

What a treat it became to read the newest drafts to
Archie. His face smoothed in repose as he listened.
Often, Belle could not tell whether he was grasping the
words or simply resting in the flow of her voice, but a
handful of times, he interrupted her by repeating a phrase
she had just shared, and a few of those times, he voiced
them with changes that Belle recognized as corrections.
She searched for a way to read and pause that would elicit
more of these adjustments, but Archie's silence remained
largely intact. Even his few changes, though, seemed
enormous. They possessed the weight of true
collaboration and firmed Belle's certainty that this was
indeed Archie's book. She considered herself his
secretary, and she was glad to be.

Sadly, there were instances of poor temper. Once
when Archie had been fiddling with a length of cord that
slipped from his fingers, Belle instinctively reached to

pick it up.

"No!" Archie said. "Leave it be!"

Belle started as if sighting a snake. Her father retrieved the cord and clutched it to his chest.

"I'm sorry, Father."

"I can do it myself!" he snapped.

But nearly instantly, his face crumpled in pain. Belle started to reach out to comfort him, but hesitated as she might with a growling dog. Her chin dropped in sorrow.

Frequently after that, Archie interrupted her manuscript reading with bitter laughs and scornful repetitions of text, as if deriding what she had written. She developed a new habit of mentally draining these barbs of their harsh sound so as to leave only the words, converting them to the pleasant echoes that Archie had made earlier in the drafting process. Following one of Archie's mocking outbursts, Belle realized that she had sifted out yet another correction. It shone for her like a pearl. *He is still here*, she thought. This was as her eye fell on the holiday window garland that she had always hung with Lily.

She told Ebenezer about these sudden gusts of temper, so unlike her father, but they remained mere hearsay until one late afternoon when Archie caught their visitor flat-footed, shortly after he had stamped snow from his shoes, hung up his coat and taken a seat by the Endicotts' cheery fire for one of Belle's readings. A droll phrase made him chuckle.

"You can smile!" Archie barked. "At my daughter!"

Ebenezer's expression flattened as if from slapping.

"Laugh like an idiot!"

"Father!"

"Simpleton!"

Lava rose in Ebenezer. "Archie!" he snapped. "How dare you— "

"Ben … please." Belle's light hand was on his arm.

Ebenezer gaped at her astounded, then shot to his feet and marched to the door.

"Ben!" called Belle.

But he seized his overcoat and hat and shut the door behind himself forcefully.

fifty-seven

Anger

Immediately, Ebenezer found himself in the path of two gentlemen walking together. His sudden appearance jolted their conversation, and they parted about him jaggedly like one rock split by another, the pieces tumbling past. As Ebenezer shot onward, he saw his own glower reflected in the wary expressions of others who he passed. They skirted away as if he carried his own foul weather, though the dimming afternoon was already wintry enough.

As so often before, he swung into The Joyful Passage, which had never seemed less so.

He burned with rage that would have articulated as: *To hell with Archie. Begone with him, the sooner the better. If he's going to die, he can very well hurry up about it. And disappear for good, thank Heaven, just as Lily has. Bless her dead soul for stepping aside so Belle will not chase after her.* The thoughts coursed through him like a tankard of ale drained on a bet.

A figure at the end of the alleyway caught Ebenezer's eye and his ire. *Her.* That same old biddy who always happened upon him here. She had paused and was returning a look as fierce as his own.

"You there!" he called, pointing and quickening his pace.

Other passers-by swung their faces toward him. One tall bones of a man halted, and Ebenezer waved him on angrily, shaking his head to convey "Not you!" With relief, Bones scurried ahead with the ribboned parcel that he carried. The old woman moved on as well, but calmly and leisurely.

"Wait!" bellowed Ebenezer. But along with Bones, she had already disappeared from view.

Ebenezer sped to the corner and around it, ready to command the old biddy again. He stopped short. No such figure was in sight, even though Bones was rapidly receding. Ebenezer's mouth fell open, everything swept from his mind. But just as quickly anger surged back into place.

"Bah!" he spat. "Humbug!"

What that, he turned full about and bypassed the end of the alley. He was far too angry to return to the shop. He set off for his factory.

fifty-eight

Sour strides

As he tromped along the streets, Ebenezer's face remained stern, and he found that the alarmed traffic continued to part before him. Holiday jollity evaporated from one expression after another, and mothers tugged their children clear of his trajectory.

Just so, he thought. He resolved from then on to

appear angry and impatient whenever he walked alone, so as to clear the way and avoid interactions—even ward off pickpockets.

He doubted that he would have to search for reasons to scowl. More and more, he felt at odds with the world and everyone, with no one sharing his views or desires in any situation. His employees never worked hard enough, quickly enough or competently enough to satisfy him. They were slow of understanding. He regretted bowing to Belle's insistence that the factory add another privy, as well as another stove for warming. Any gratitude from the workers was short-lived, and his generosity seemed only to whet their greed and spur indolence. Just that week, a pair of employees claiming to speak for the majority of their mates had approached him about increases in wages.

"Out of the question," he replied. "Each job has an established payment, and there is a schedule for reevaluation. That comes on June the First, and this is December. That is the end of it."

"Respectfully, sir," said Tom Neely, the persistently calm and polite primary spokesman, "no wages changed after the reevaluation last June the First."

"Because I saw no need."

"Costs are rising for everything, sir—food, clothes, coal."

"I am aware. Increases are moderate. Why does that matter?"

"It makes life harder, sir."

"Yes, but what is the relevance to this business?"

"We are your workers, sir."

"And you have your wages."

"Is not the work to your satisfaction, sir?"

"Certainly. Our manufacturing processes ensure it."

"And the people in the processes, sir."

"Yes, of course, but people come and go. The processes remain and improve."

"We are not simply parts in a machine, sir—gears to wear out and replace."

"From the perspective of the business, you are indeed. The process is fashioned for particular roles, not particular people. If it did, what would happen if, Heaven forbid, you, Mr. Neely, or any particular person, were trampled by a horse? No worker can be irreplaceable."

"But a particular worker can be awfully hard to do without."

"Actually, that is not true."

"No, sir?"

"No. You have worked here long enough to see me replace skilled and unskilled workers alike. I have to take the perspective of the business, and the business must never rely excessively on any worker. Naturally, different roles pay differently. The more rare the qualifications, the higher the pay. But I never look at myself as hiring a person, only filling a role. And I am not shy about this: I will always pay as little as necessary for any role. That is simply good business. When I do not change wages, it is because the value of that role in the broader economy has not changed. The market sets the price, and I adhere to it. I am pleased to report, from the perspective of the business, that no price for any of our roles has risen in the past year."

"So there is no reward for experience in the role, sir?"

"Each role has its specific minimum capability. There is no reward for excessive capability."

"Excessive capability means doing more than the role requires?"

"Yes. Rewarding that would be foolish. The work needs to be as good as required and no better."

"So improvement does not matter?"

"Improvement of the role or the process matters."

"Is there reward for that, then, sir? Finding ways for improvement?"

"That is my role. Or one of my roles. As I observe the work, I ponder new ways to go about it, and I propose them or require them."

"And if we, the fillers of the roles, have any ideas for improvement?"

"I cannot rely on that, but I would like to have these ideas, of course. I did just that for my final employer. When I had suggestions, I made them."

"And were you rewarded for your suggestions, sir?"

Ebenezer hedged here. "At times, yes. And it was a mistake."

Fezziwig had indeed given Ebenezer a bounty on occasion, when he voiced particular insights that led to productive new practices. "You are the goose that lays the golden eggs, my boy!" he had proclaimed. "It would be foolish not to feed you well and try to keep you in my barn!" As grateful as Ebenezer had been for these gifts, they also made him somewhat embarrassed for his master. He frequently found Fezziwig overly generous, and he considered this shortsightedness. Yes, Fezziwig had done well, but Ebenezer often mused how much more successful he might have been if he had not so often wasted his money.

"Not I," Ebenezer muttered as he hurried along, recalling this conversation with Neely, which he had quickly brought to an end. "Not I, not I, not I. Never, never, never."

"Never?"

He heard the voice just as he was about to collide with the person speaking. Here was one man who was not ducking from his path. In fact, he had deliberately stood in the way.

It was Marley.

"Never," said Scrooge. He found his mood marginally lifted. McHugh had told him that Marley liked him, and he had sensed the man's genuine admiration after their one brief encounter. He now found himself interested in this Door Knocker of a character.

"Tell me more?" said Marley, pointing to a nearby pub. "My treat?"

"Never," said Scrooge "...would I refuse your offer to pay. Thank you."

"Splendid," said Marley.

fifty-nine

In the pub

"Now then," said Marley in their booth in the pub, "care to tell me what you were muttering about? And scowling about?"

Much to his surprise, Scrooge did. He told Marley everything up to the minute about his manufacturing business and Classic Buttons, then worked backward to Fezziwig and his own thorough self-education. This was interwoven with Marley's tracing his own background, from his drunkard father to his years as a roustabout and barman, then a tavern owner.

"Served as my own bouncer," said Marley.

"Bouncer?" said Scrooge. "What is that?"

"Don't you know the term?"

Scrooge shook his head.

Marley looked toward the street and grinned at catching sight of something. He glanced at the barman, just then occupied chatting with a curvy maiden. "Watch this," Marley said, with a wink, sliding from his seat. In three long strides, he was at the door intercepting two stylishly-dressed young men just then entering. He planted his feet and raised his beefy palms to the pair, leaning into them with a glare. Surprised, they halted.

"Out," Marley said, pointing to the street. His order was quiet but laced with menace and brought immediate obedience. The pair retreated without a word.

Marley turned back to Scrooge, making a show of clapping his palms clean, and resumed his seat.

"That's bouncing?" asked Scrooge.

"That's bouncing," said Marley.

"Never laid eyes on them before?"

"Never."

Scrooge raised his glass. "Well done."

Marley clinked the glass and shrugged. "It's a gift."

"How did you bounce from bouncing to banking?"

"Every establishment requires banking. And my own banker saw something in me. Casper was his name."

"He saw your inner banker?"

"No, he saw his future collector."

"Ah, yes. Go around and get the money owed."

"Exactly. It was on commission, and when I heard the percentages to be had from collections, and the amounts of the collections, I sold the tavern in a wink and set about making easy money. I had a way of showing up at a place of business and blocking the light, if you take my meaning."

"The money just fell from the pockets."

"Flew out like birds, the pound notes did."

"Before anything bad happened."

"Rarely got that far, but I always encouraged the belief that things might turn unpleasant."

The men held the booth long into the evening,

ultimately ordering dinner and three pints apiece, each of them twice having to excuse himself to use the privy. Ebenezer grew giddy. He found Marley a kindred spirit remarkably in line with his thinking in many areas, while sharply divergent in others, culminating with his intention to marry Belle.

"She'll just slow you down," Marley scoffed. "And cost you. Look at how she's already fouled up your button works. Extra stove, extra privy. Extra bother, extra expense."

"True, true."

"So yank 'em back out."

"I've thought of it."

"Will you?"

"Not tonight," Scrooge joked.

"Tomorrow, then."

"If I choose."

"How will you do it?"

"Do what?"

"Remove the privy."

"I haven't said I will."

"You will."

"You've decided?"

"No, you have."

Ebenezer looked at him mindfully. "And the stove?"

"Out." Marley repeated his grave tone of expulsion from earlier and arced a thumb toward the street.

Scrooge looked at him for ticks of the clock.

"Tell me more of my future?" he said.

sixty

Approprio

Marley leaned back and peered at him as if appraising a thoroughbred. The gaze lingered. Scrooge appeared content to wait through the night for the reply. Finally, Marley gave a slight nod and spoke.

"Approprio."

"Approprio?"

"Approprio."

"Is that Italian?"

"Latin."

"You are a devotee of the ancient tongue?"

"Only have a few words, but that's one of 'em. Casper the Banker gave it to me."

"And you are giving it to me."

"Yes."

"Why?"

"Same reason Casper gave it to me. It's who you are."

"Approprio," said Scrooge, tasting the word again. "Root word of 'appropriate?' Meaning 'proper'?"

"And 'appropriate,'" said Marley, making the final syllable 'ate.'

"Meaning 'take.'"

"Meaning to make one's own, *ad proprius*. That, Scrooge, is what you were made to do. Make things your own. It's the only proper, appropriate use of your life."

"Quite a pronouncement."

"Because I know you. I am you. Casper was the same. He saw it in me, I see it in you. You asked me your future, that is the answer. You will appropriate."

"Take."

"Make your own, man! It's the smallest and the biggest difference. To take is to steal, to thieve, to force loss upon another. That's not what we do, you and I. It's not proper, so it's exactly the opposite of what we do. We make our own. Yes, property transfers to us—'property' comes from the same root word, by the way, *proprius*— but not by force, not by crime. Everything within the law. Proper. This is in your blood. I saw it plain as day in that contract you wrote for the button shop. You wrote it within the law to make it your own, given the correct circumstances. *Approprio*."

"Approprio." The word spun from Scrooge's tongue with a spark of recognition even as the liquid spirits danced in his blood.

"I don't know about this woman," said Marley. "I warn you against her. I say that she is not for you. But I do know this: I am."

"You," said Scrooge with a light laugh.

"Me. We will be partners in business. I am appropriating you."

"Taking m— "

"Making," Marley growled.

" —making me your own."

"It's as simple as that, sir. You and I are bound in this life. And perhaps after. I know it in my soul."

"Marley and Scrooge."

"Or Scrooge and Marley if you like, I don't care a whit."

"I do like that better."

"But it is as plain as fate to me, man. You and I are bound by chains."

"Ghastly."

"Horrifying," Marley raised his pint. "But true."

Scrooge raised his. They clinked glasses and said it again together:

"*Approprio*."

sixty-one

Wandering

They agreed that Marley would come to the button factory the following day to give it a good look and provide his assessment.

"Until then," Marley said, departing with his typical two-fingered salute.

Ebenezer doubted that he would sleep that night, so stirred was he, and he commenced an aimless stroll. He placed his steps carefully as the day tumbled through his mind and he gauged his degree of inebriation, both from the pints and from the currents and cross-currents coursing through his life.

He decided to avoid Classic Buttons and made a point of routing himself toward his boyhood home. Not to walk there—it was much too distant—but to orient his thinking. He grounded himself in the fundamentals of his existence: His father. Fan. Books. Work. Fezziwig. Business. Buttons. Belle. Archie.

Belle. He found the button in his pocket. Her time with Lily was concluded. She was soon to lose Archie. She would wear mourning dress. He pictured her, somber and trim in grey and black. Her story in coming days, conveyed to all by her clothing, would be her loss. For months, for years, it would define her as a person who had lost a person.

He knew more of her than that. She was an author. Her book was quite good. It would be a valuable resource on a vanished trade. As the writing had progressed, Ebenezer had marveled at the change in his position relative to a literary work. He had known countless books, but only as an outsider. Their authors were vital figures in his life, but forever unseen—communicative but vaporous. Knowledgeable phantoms. Now he stood and sat and walked beside and leaned against and joked with and embraced and kissed an author in magnificent flesh and fervent blood. She was producing a book, and he was there to see the creation, as inside a collection of pages as he would ever be. Even though she would never mention him in her writing, he was part of her story and she part of his.

As now was Marley. *Approprio.*

Her shop, thought Ebenezer, *I will appropriate it—make it my own. Her insistence on adding a privy and stove at the factory—I made those notions my own, but now I will reject them.*

How circuitous that was: He was coming to own everything that Belle possessed—making her life his own. The opposite was also true. As husband and wife, they would own each other's lives. She could make suggestions, and they would become his to ignore or act upon and sometimes undo as he chose. And the same would be true of his suggestions to her: She could take them or leave them—make them her own or not. She would become his … property? And he hers? How could he make anything his own if he did not even own his decisions and himself? Marriage ceremonies spoke of two becoming one flesh. But there would still be the two of them, and he must remain his own.

His throat tightened as he thought of expressing any of this to Belle. His decisions in their life would be doings of business, and he could only ever trust his own judgment. He had no doubt she would not understand. She would be hurt when he reversed her urgings at the factory, failing to see that it was crucial to his regaining his grasp on the employees and their expectations. They must know their place, and his. And she must know her own place.

Her shop—making it his own place. Appropriating it.

Exercising his proper self. Her place no longer her place, but now his place. His place beside her—and not.

His stomach clenched, and he stopped walking. He looked about and came to himself with a start. Despite his intentions, he was just up the walk from Classic Buttons, at the mouth of The Joyful Passage. Intending the opposite, nevertheless here he was. He pivoted toward the alley but did not enter, simply staring into the dark void.

"Belle," he breathed.

He was exhausted and empty. Groaning, he turned for home.

sixty-two

Restless waiting

At the moment of this turning away by her fiancé, Belle rolled over in her bed. She had yet to sleep. Archie's agitation earlier in the day had been short-lived, lasting only long enough to repel Ebenezer, but the tumult had continued in her mind.

Why had he not returned? Belle certainly understood his storming out. Archie's outbursts were cutting. She had often felt the lash. Her own response was to be soothing, to hush her father, to smooth his hair, embrace him, rock him back into tranquility. Somehow she knew that these explosions were one of Archie's few ways of communicating his anguish and distress. His mind no longer functioned, and his strength was ebbing. He was a wounded animal, a frightened child, capable only of silence or snarling.

"My dear boy," she whispered. "My dear little Archie."

Now many evenings wound down this way, daughter cradling father. On the days that she bathed him, his clean soap smell enhanced her pleasure in holding him. He was a wobbling creature, dependent, finding peace in her arms. Her past became this present and future. She was daughter, companion and mother. It was the best and worst of times.

That evening, after Archie calmed and let Belle tuck him into bed with a final kiss to his forehead, she stood at the window watching for Ebenezer, finally abandoning that post to complete more writing for her book— Archie's book—by lamplight. The least sound would send her to the window, where she would find nothing, and she would resume her work. She repeated this cycle until her head started to droop and her ink lines waggled in fatigue. She prepared for bed and lay down.

"Father in Heaven," she whispered. "Father in Heaven, Father in Heaven."

As she drowsed, she added "Mother in Heaven" and "Father and Mother in Heaven," drifting between the variations.

She lay in prayerful repose, lolling and coming back awake. At times she heard footfalls outside, or thought she did. Such was the way on their street.

There! Was that a familiar stride? A groan?

"Ebenezer," she breathed. But no, it was too late for him. She lay still. She slept.

sixty-three

Early arrival

Ebenezer did not sleep. He laid awake thinking through what he would do at the factory. He was not long in his bed. The clock had scarcely struck the new day before he rose and lit a lamp and scrubbed himself with cold water. He dressed with utmost care and purposely left the red button on its hook, not even glancing at it.

Just before closing the door on his way out, he paused, turned back for the button, but then stopped himself and continued on his way.

Yes, Dear Reader, he left me behind. But whatever allows me to know what I know and tell it to you—that force has never abated. Those of you who know Scrooge from other writing might recall a fireplace in his home constructed with tiles possibly capable of reflecting his thoughts and experiences. Perhaps these tiles displayed his comings and goings, perhaps they did not. I will say this: I was hung in line with just such a fireplace. Now then …

Through floating snow, Ebenezer strode briskly toward his building. It was easy to wear the grim face that he had resolved to maintain while in transit. This day, he would be as severe as granite. His agenda rose before him like a set of steps. Upward he would march.

Inside the factory, he visited each spot that he would tread in the coming hours, and he projected forward to what he would see and say.

Here in the doorway of his office is where he would beckon his factory manager and hand him a diagram for clearing a large open space on the floor.

Here in that space is where all of the workers would assemble—an extraordinary measure that would make everyone whisper in speculation.

Here at the side of the space is where he would direct Marley to stand. At the time that he and Scrooge had set for his arrival, all of the workers would just then have finished gathering.

Here at the front of that space is where Scrooge would instruct the manager to fashion a platform by placing a sturdy table next to the set of portable steps used about the factory for reaching shelves. For practice, Scrooge climbed the steps and quickly saw that he would want two tables rather than one, aligned on their long sides and temporarily affixed by boards nailed across the tables' shorter edges. He pulled two tables together to confirm this, remounted and nodded in satisfaction. Yes, much better. The elevation briefly made him think of looking up at Belle as she occupied his tall desk, but he shook away the image. He paced on the tables and mentally rehearsed the points that he would orate.

Welcome Marley as a guest (a studious banker)
Explain: He's learning about this business … This morning will bring him up to the moment
Call Tom Neely forward
Dismiss him from employment
Summon the shop steward to see Neely out
Explain: This is because Neely was your spokesman for higher wages
Explain what I discussed with Neely: Processes over people (simplified)
Explain my lesson learned: Sudden changes here created confusion
Explain: I must restore clarity with a compensating set of changes ("curative" might be a better word)
These curative changes, to be executed today, are:
1. Removing the new privy

2. Removing the new stove
Explain: I led you to equate work with comfort …
A mistake (precisely modulate this admission)
Drive home: Work is a MEANS to comfort

Inhabiting this scenario, Ebenezer shifted into speaking aloud.

"If I make these surroundings too comfortable, I will remind you of your homes, where you have liberty to be idle and merry. I don't make myself merry when I work, and I can't afford to make idle people merry.

"If you are somewhat eager to leave your work at the end of the day, so much the better. Hasten to your families. Eat, drink, rest, renew, return.

"My fondest wish for you is not comfort at work. It is work that makes you forget comfort. That is what I find: I become so caught up in what I do that I forget to eat. When my blood is stirred I need no fire, no food, not even a seat—that is why I now stand at my desk and save the time of moving a chair. Manufacture your own comfort, and you construct something far more valuable than buttons. That is your true work.

"Return to that now, and remember these lessons."

Yes, yes, yes, that would do well.

Scrooge stepped down from the tables and returned the second one to its place, as well as the steps. Pleased with himself, he felt in his pocket for the button. He halted in the dim emptiness of the floor, distraught at its absence, then recalled that he had left it behind in his flat. Thoughts quickly followed: *Belle will not know of this day. Just as well. Impossible, anyway: She cannot leave Archie now. Good. But he won't last long. Pity.*

Ebenezer shook his head at his own callousness, then steeled himself. *Bah!* These musings must end. Business demanded it.

sixty-four

Workplace address

Everything occurred just as Scrooge imagined. No, even better. It was all crisp and exhilarating. The speaking platform came together quickly. The whispers of the workers seemed to him like the tuning of an orchestra before a concert.

Marley arrived precisely at the time agreed. He looked about and cocked an eyebrow at the scene. Scrooge gave him a confident grin and shook his hand. "I'm seizing opportunity," Scrooge said. "You shall see."

"Devil," said Marley with a wink.

"I'll introduce you as a banker and interested party."

"Not by name, please." At Scrooge's puzzled look, he added. "I'll explain later."

Scrooge nodded and put it out of his mind.

Atop the stage, words snapped from his tongue. Each face turned up to him was small and transfixed. He drew his employees' attention and tugged their thoughts as if with strings. He saw astonishment ripple through them when he expelled Neely, and their wary gazes made him feel no less than godlike. They were souls at his command. So strong did he feel in his delivery that he triumphantly flicked his eyes once toward Marley, and he found the man's face glowing with approval. This spurred him into his climactic words, then he dispersed the assembled as the wind scatters dandelion puffs.

He beamed at Marley as he descended the steps and grasped the hand extended.

"Bravo, sir," said Marley. "You seized opportunity indeed."

"Thank you," said Scrooge. "I am merely executing what you predicted."

"But I never foresaw this flair. And on a hangover,

yet. Imagine what you could do sober. Well done." Marley had leaned in with these final words, and Scrooge flinched at his foul breath. Marley noticed and chuckled.

"Beg pardon. Perhaps you have some mint I could chew, in your office?"

"Sadly not."

"Show your office to me still?" His manner conveyed that he wanted to communicate something in private.

Closing Scrooge's door, Marley immediately said, "Call in Usstin."

"My salesman? You know him?"

"Salesman, is he?"

"My selling representative. He has become the supervisor of my other two."

"Who are they?"

"Jonson and Sincello. They each knew Usstin separately before they began working for me, and they recommended him. He's done marvelously. The sales keep growing."

"Are Jonson and Sincello present as well?"

"No, they go directly to their sales routes. They'll be in this afternoon."

"I see. So for now, Usstin. Call him in."

"But why? You haven't answered me about knowing him. What is he to you?"

"Trust me, it will become clear."

After the briefest pause, Scrooge opened the door and made the summons.

sixty-five

An employee's past

Shortly, Usstin appeared.

"You wanted to see me, sir?"

Scrooge waved him in. Usstin nodded at Marley.

"Jerome Usstin," he said, extending his hand. Marley took it.

"Jacob Marley," he said.

Usstin started. Marley kept hold of his hand and tightened his grip. Now Scrooge saw why Marley had not wanted his name announced to the workers.

"What's your scheme this time?" Marley said.

Usstin kept silent, his face tight with distress.

"I'll find out, you know," Marley said. "It won't go well for you." He squeezed harder.

"Nothing!" blurted Usstin as he writhed. "No scheme!"

"Just selling, eh?"

"I swear."

"Then you won't mind taking me to your customers."

Usstin blanched around wide eyes.

"Ah, you do mind," Marley said. He tightened his grip, and Usstin fought not to yelp.

"I'll find out," Marley repeated. "Feel like telling me?"

After a jot more resistance, Usstin nodded.

Marley released him, and Usstin's face collapsed in relief. He gingerly waggled feeling back into his hand.

"Simply put, Scrooge," Marley said, "Usstin here is a criminal. We have never met, as you have gathered, but he knows my name from a past incident. In my days as a debt collector, I visited a builder of homes who had fallen behind on payments because his most recent client turned out to have none of the wealth that he pretended to.

This builder had been convinced by appearances: exquisite clothing and wigs and a carriage, not to mention the client's bonny wife with her parasol. The lady did have a way with a parasol. This shining couple also had a bashful teenage footman—Mr. Usstin here, who happened to be the son of the swindler. The lovely young wife was the elder Usstin's niece, from another branch of this family of thieves.

"It was a fronting scheme—the Usstins had enough money to purchase the site of construction and to acquire their finery, all toward demonstrating the means to afford their grand new home. Beyond this, they had wolfish wiles—a sinister expertise in nudging persons of business from their usual cautions and practice. The builder was sorely embarrassed to admit to me that he had fallen under the charms of the Usstins and funded all of the materials and labor for the new home in an attempt to expedite the project, dispensing with his usual insistence on initial and periodic payments. He was astonished at himself. I came to understand why: Usstin Senior was a beguiling fellow, and the niece was magnetic. I learned this firsthand when I went around to visit them on behalf of the builder as well as my own banker. I glimpsed young Usstin here through one of the richly-appointed windows, but even from afar I could see lively energy as he gamboled with a waif in the courtyard. Hardly the shy youth that he portrayed.

"I had the pleasure of expelling these vipers from their opulent den. We foreclosed and took possession through the court, which also seized their land as punishment. I ultimately sold the home for a handsome sum and did all I could to restore the builder, a most kindly gentleman and former military officer with distinguished service. He was far too stalwart, intelligent and disciplined to have aided any of his own misfortune, and yet he had. The Usstins are masters of manipulation.

"Let me ask you straightforwardly, Scrooge. Has Mr. Usstin here moved you away from safeguards that you would normally have taken?"

In horrific increments, this is exactly what had been dawning on Scrooge. He nodded without expression.

"Usstin's customers. Have you met them? Visited them?"

Scrooge shook his head.

"But they've paid their bills?"

"Without fail. Even before they were due."

"Always through Usstin?"

"Yes. All of the receipts have matched the orders."

"Sizable orders, from what you've said."

"And growing, for months."

"Good customers," Marley said, turning to Usstin, "that you don't want us to visit with you. Why would that be?"

Usstin made a brief show of not responding, staring straight ahead. Marley stepped toward him.

"Tell me."

It was the same uncanny chilling voice that he had demonstrated at the tavern, and Usstin was instantly shaken from his recalcitrance.

"Because they're not customers."

"But the orders," said Scrooge. "The payments."

"Where did the money come from?" said Marley.

Usstin licked his lips, reluctant to answer, but knowing he would.

"Mercer."

Scrooge's balance wobbled as if he'd taken a dart to the forehead. From his throat came a burst of laughter.

Mercer! The maker of fabric and clothing. A giant enterprise with massive buildings, hundreds of tailors and thousands of sewers turning out garments for all of

Britain. Gloves, pants, stockings, shirts, jackets, on and on for men, women, boys, girls, babies. A thriving exporter as well.

Scrooge laughed again in disbelief. It was as ludicrous as suddenly tasting sugar in the air after wishing for it for months. Mercer was ever present in his mind. The company was a paramount concern, a feared competitor. He had in fact sought to make them a customer. Upon forming his business, one of his earliest efforts was seeking an introduction to principals at Mercer. He had not reached the owner or primary figures, but he did speak to an elevated level of manager. Scrooge elaborated enthusiastically on the advantage that he could offer, holding forward that the finest supply would come from a company such as his, which concentrated only on manufacturing buttons. It was too intricate an art, he insisted, to add to Mercer's other pursuits, which already included spinning thread, looming fabric, printing patterns, and myriad other stages of creating garments.

The Mercer man had thrown cold water on Scrooge's fire, dismissing him politely but succinctly. "We wish you well," he had said, "but we have other sources."

Scrooge had visited dozens of other garment-makers: Large concerns such as Hartman & McMasters, Workinger and Sward, and later approaching smaller tailor shops. He received additional spurnings but gained enough accounts to move forward. It was after this that he recruited sales representatives to further bolster his roster of customers. Now he found that one of those representatives had connected his little company to the behemoth Mercer after all, but in a sinister way. Here was the perfidious industrial espionage that he despised and had dreaded.

"Mercer," said Scrooge, surging toward Usstin. "Why?" His own growl was as fearsome as Marley's, and

Usstin shrank away. "Where are the buttons you delivered?"

"They're warehoused, for now."

"For now? What happens later? What is their plan?"

"To drive you from business," said Usstin, "and gain your assets for a pittance."

Scrooge's blood ran cold. "Because that income will vanish," he whispered, as if to himself. Internally, he continued the thought: *I won't be able to cover my costs. I'll lose my equipment, my building, my inventory. Everything.*

IV

sixty-six

A decisive response

In years to come, when Marley told the story, he would swear that when Scrooge fell motionless in the office just then, the room instantly chilled. In the earliest tellings, Marley said that the cooling was merely perceptible. Over time, this became a drop of five degrees. After a decade, it was ten degrees. After another decade, Marley claimed that frost settled on every surface, and icicles dangled from the ceiling.

"That's when you aged," Marley would also say, snapping his fingers. "Instantly becoming an old miser like me, or even older. My elder brother from another mother."

"Bah," Scrooge would reply, mocking his own masterfully-deployed ill temper. "Humbug."

But with instant aging came instant wisdom, Marley would add, and he meant it. As hard as the partners became on each other—constant needling that occasionally burst into roaring battles that made their clerk shudder—they shared deep mutual respect. Part of this stemmed back to Scrooge's swift actions upon discovering Usstin's subterfuge.

Scrooge turned toward the window that faced the production floor. He was motionless.

Marley crossed his arms and leaned against the wall. Usstin worked at staying still and becoming invisible.

A minute passed. Five. Ten. Fifteen. Usstin dared a glance at Marley, who gave him a slow wink that Usstin found unnerving.

At long last, Scrooge turned back. His spine was straight, his jaw firm, his eyes gleaming like jewels.

"You shall wait here," he said to Usstin. "You shall come with me," he said to Marley.

Scrooge closed the door behind them. Through the window, Usstin watched the pair confer. Scrooge calmly but energetically imparted an explanation to Marley, who bent in close attention. At points Marley curled back in surprise, and once his head arced over in a clear expression of disbelief, but Scrooge remained cool and adamant, and he came to gesture in all directions, seeming to indicate intentions involving spots both within and outside of the factory. Soon Marley was leaning in again, nodding in understanding. Ultimately, he grasped Scrooge's shoulder and gave it a squeeze as they shook hands and exchanged a few final words.

The men re-entered the room and closed the door.

"Now then," said Scrooge. "Your final delivery to Mercer."

Usstin swallowed.

" ... will be delayed. We will keep you comfortable while you wait. Marley will stay close to you and see to your needs."

"Need the privy?" Marley said to Usstin.

Usstin shook his head.

"Drink of water?"

Another head shake.

"I'll check with you again in a bit. For now, follow me."

Usstin rose.

"Bring your chair," Marley said. Usstin numbly obeyed.

Marley led him out to Scrooge's makeshift platform and up the steps. He pointed to the center of the space.

"Sit," he said.

Usstin placed his chair and sat. Marley returned to the floor without another word.

Naturally, the other employees looked over quizzically at Usstin. He did his best to fix a gaze over their heads and betray none of his befuddlement and panic. It caught his eye when Scrooge summoned the factory manager to his office—his elevated perch gave him a perfect angle on this. The manager soon exited and beckoned his lieutenants and gave them brief instruction. These latter spread through the workers and herded them again toward the stage. The equipment fell silent, and the workers, puzzled and murmuring, gathered for the second time that day. Marley resumed his place at the wall. Scrooge made his way back onto the stage and stood to one side of Usstin.

"It is an extraordinary day," Scrooge said. "Our first full-scale gathering as a company was earlier this morning. Already, here is another. I know that I am trying your patience and straining your understanding, but I beg your indulgence. I will be brief.

"I cannot give a full explanation now, but I will as soon as possible. We will gather yet again later today, and then I will tell you all that I can. There will be much activity in the time between. What I will say for now might seem confounding, but perhaps less so if I tell all of you at once in this way. I ask you to simply accept what you do understand and set aside the rest for now. I implore you to cooperate with me and with those who will aid me.

"I am asking for your help to allow the continued growth and health of this enterprise. That was also the intent of my earlier remarks, but this second gathering concerns different matters entirely. As soon as our first assembly concluded, I learned some information that exploded particular understandings. As dramatic as that sounds, it is also accurate. Things quickly reassembled in my mind and came to compose a plan. That is what we will implement as follows:

"Our chief sales representative, Mr. Usstin, will remain here on the platform. Later, you will learn why. For now, I will say that he will engage in contemplation.

"He will be aided by the visitor who I briefly introduced earlier but whose name I neglected to share. This is Mr. Jacob Marley."

Marley raised his hand to present himself.

" … who has great interest in our company and lends valuable insight.

"This afternoon, our other sales representatives, Misters Jonson and Sincello, will join Mr. Usstin on this platform. All three will be kept comfortable—provided food and escorted to the privy and so forth.

"As you know, the three of them have had incredible success in acquiring orders. They are due special recognition."

Here Scrooge began light applause, and the workers confusedly followed suit. Marley clapped heartily. Usstin's expression wavered between stolidity and mortification, and he finally gave a slight nod.

"All of you," continued Scrooge, "are engaged in preparing the largest order to date. In part to signify this milestone, all three of the sales representatives will transport the order together. Please apply yourselves to completing the entire amount by the end of day." This directive made concern ripple through the workers.

"I know this is asking much of you," said Scrooge, raising his voice to quell the murmur. "We had allowed more time for the work, but the schedule must accelerate. The aforementioned extra stove and extra privy are yet at hand. I reaffirm my earlier announcements about removing them, but at present it is fitting that these remain available for your comfort. Because of the size of the order, I expect to ask you to stay beyond your usual finishing time—any who are able. You will receive extra wages commensurate with this, and I will also send for food and drink." This happy announcement brought a wave of smiles.

"And one more thing," said Scrooge, "that might seem the most remarkable of all."

The workers fell silent and looked at him expectantly.

"Later in the day, a musician will be at hand."

The workers buzzed in surprise.

"As well as a writer of songs. You will see this person on the premises composing through the day, but at times the musician will play for you, to make your extra work more pleasant."

The excited ripple quickened, though some employees held wary expressions.

"If all goes well," continued Scrooge, "you will hear a completed composition by late afternoon.

"To reiterate, my explanation for all of this is forthcoming. Until then, thank you for your diligence and faith. I implore you to work with alacrity."

There were smatterings of applause as Scrooge

dismounted. Marley gave him another handshake and clap on the shoulder.

"Now to acquire a musician and a songwriter," said Scrooge, his brow furrowed.

"Not to worry," said Marley. "You already know an excellent fiddler."

"You?"

"No, no, certainly not. I mean our mutual friend."

In a trice, Scrooge realized who this must be. "McHugh?"

"The same. He's masterful. And believe it or not, his wife is a rare hand at the guitar."

"Is she?"

"I expect you could enlist both of them."

"I'll go see McHugh at once, if you don't mind standing by here."

"Not at all. Do you happen to know a songwriter?"

"I do have someone in mind. I shall also visit her."

"Her," said Marley, a light dawning in his eyes.

"Her," said Scrooge.

sixty-seven

The affianced confer

Belle sat stunned.

Only moments before, Ebenezer had finally reappeared. He made an earnest apology for his abrupt departure and prolonged absence, and she promptly forgave him. This had immediately flowed into Ebenezer's measured description of the calamity that had befallen his enterprise and on to his explanation—admission— that because of the language of the contract with Classic

Buttons, her father's shop—her very home—was also at stake.

She ceased motion for so long that Ebenezer came to wonder if she had fallen into one of her reveries with her mother, even though he understood these to have discontinued. As if intuiting his thought, Belle reached out and touched his sleeve.

"For better, for worse," she said, still not looking at him.

"For richer, for poorer," he said.

Finally she turned to him.

"This is much to take in, Ben. I'm frightened. I must say that I question your judgment regarding father's home. It angers me, to be honest. I am struggling to understand."

"I will not lose your home, Belle. I promise you."

"It is Father's home. I'm not afraid for myself, but I feel you have put him at risk."

"I will not lose his home, Belle. I swear to you. I will save this business and mine. We will save them. I need your help."

"How?"

He detailed his plan. The shifts in her expression were as swift and indescribable as changes in a cloud. She shook her head in wonder.

"You will save it all with a song?"

"With a song, Belle, yes, we will. If you will write it."

"I am barely a writer at all."

"And I barely a businessman."

"Barely a businessman. Look at all you have done."

"Look at all I have done. Brought us to the brink."

"That is not what I— "

"I know. Nevertheless, this is when I will prove myself. Today. I have to believe that."

"I've already told you that you have nothing to prove

to me. And that I believe in you."

"In us."

"Us."

He remained silent.

"Ben, look at me." He met her gaze.

"When your desperate plan succeeds—and I say when, not if, because I know that it shall—will that be sufficient proof? Will you believe yourself worthy then? Will anything ever be enough?"

Ebenezer closed his eyes. "I cannot think about that now. I know you ask the question in love, but— "

She took his hand. "Let us come back to it."

"Yes."

She took a deep breath. "I will write your song."

"Thank you."

She leaned in and kissed him.

"I love you," she said.

"Despite all of this."

"Within all of this."

Belle looked toward Archie's room, where he was still sleeping.

"I'll have to bring him with me," she said.

"Of course, and he is welcome."

"I cannot promise that he will behave himself."

"I know that he can't help it. On my honor, I am prepared for anything that he might say."

"I'll get him up and dressed, and we'll be there as soon as we can."

"Take your time. McHugh will not be at the factory for a while yet. And I have to make another stop or two, including to arrange the food and drink for everyone."

"The expense will pierce your soul, Ebenezer Scrooge."

"Don't you know my reputation?" he returned in kind. "I have no soul."

sixty-eight

Converging on the factory

After arranging for the food and drink and wincing at the cost beneath a stiff nod of thanks, Scrooge hurried back to the factory. McHugh was already there, releasing a light air with his fiddle. This contributed to a hum on the factory floor unlike any Scrooge had seen. He could only shake his head at the fact that Usstin held the stage in his chair, under the bemused watch of Marley, as if a compulsory master of this ceremony.

McHugh came to the end of his tune, and Scrooge applauded lightly, then warmly shook the hand of his banker.

"Marley spoke truly of your skill," Scrooge said even as the Door Knocker himself approached.

"You are too kind," said McHugh, giving a slight bow.

"For today perhaps I am," said Scrooge. "I will reform at the first opportunity." He gestured to his office. "May we confer?"

The three of them talked vigorously even as Marley continued to keep an eye on the stone-faced Usstin.

The discussion dissolved at the appearance of Belle and Archie, the latter shuffling in pale, puny and pitiful. Scrooge introduced them in all directions.

"I've heard much about you," said Marley, bowing gallantly to Belle. "Ebenezer speaks most highly."

"How nice to meet you, Mr. Marley."

"Hello, Mr. Endicott," Marley said to her father, boosting his volume.

"Archie, please," said Archie huskily.

"I'm Jacob. I work with Ebenezer."

"Beezer."

"Yes, Beezer."

"And this is James," said Scrooge, indicating McHugh.

"Fiddle," said Archie, his withered hand darting toward McHugh's instrument.

"Yes!" said McHugh, raising the fiddle for a skim with his bow.

Instantly, Archie's eyes took on a shine. Belle gasped with delight and swung an imploring look at McHugh, who nodded and launched into what would clearly be the first of many offerings. Archie stood in rapture, but only briefly, because a young workman hurried over with two stools for father and daughter. Scrooge took care to thank him.

"Beg pardon, sir," said the lad, "but my uncle lives just a skip away. I could run over and borrow a rocking chair for the old gent. He'd be more comfortable."

"That would be most kind," Scrooge said.

In a flash the boy returned with the rocker.

Belle extended her hand to him. "Devon, isn't it?" She summoned his name from her earlier visit to the factory.

"You remembered, Miss Belle!"

"I do, and I cannot thank you enough, Devon. Would you mind terribly if I gave you a hug for your thoughtfulness?"

"Not at all, Miss Belle!"

Young Devon fairly glided back to his work.

Archie rocked happily as McHugh played. Belle beamed at Scrooge, who nodded in return.

"Now then," he said, "would you like to write right here, next to Archie? We can find a small table for you."

"That will be perfect."

McHugh did not break from playing until his wife Carlotta arrived. After she was introduced all around, her singing and guitar playing provided fresh delight to

Archie and the busy workers.

At mid-day, Jonson and Sincello arrived. Their eyes went wide at the tableau greeting them. They proceeded from astonishment to abasement during an extended interview with Scrooge and Marley in the former's office. After this, Marley united them with Usstin on the stage, which had earlier been doubled with the addition of two more tables. Each was seated at arm's-length from Usstin, facing away from him and therefore each other. Through the afternoon, each was kept comfortable with water and use of the privy.

Between smiling drowses and prolonged naps, Archie remained captivated by the music. At times, he shriveled into tears, and Belle knelt at his side to comfort him. These bouts of melancholy soon passed, and his murmuring told her that he was steeped in happy nostalgia.

"The older the songs the better, if you don't mind," Belle remarked to Carlotta, to whom she had instantly sparked.

"Play all the favorites," said Carlotta to McHugh, who grinned.

"How's the writing coming?" he asked Belle.

"Quite well, I think. I'll soon be ready to show something to Ben."

"Ben?" said McHugh.

"Sorry, Ebenezer. Ben is a pet name."

"How darling!" said Carlotta.

"Good ol' Ben Scrooge," said McHugh, launching into the next tune.

sixty-nine

A friend with a press

Scrooge spent an uncomfortably long time considering her verses, Belle thought as he perused them from on high at his standing desk, only the two of them in his office.

Finally, he looked up, his stern expression giving way to a smile.

"Brilliant."

"Yes?"

"Yes, darling. Just what I wanted. Thank you."

Theatrically, Belle sighed and wiped her brow.

"Let's call in the others," said Scrooge.

They gathered when Archie's next nap allowed both Carlotta and McHugh to be at hand, along with Marley. Carlotta sang while McHugh played an old familiar tune to which Belle had set her lyrics.

Smiles bloomed all about. The song delivered just the burst that Scrooge had sought.

"The perfect carol," he declared. "Thank you, Miss Endicott."

Amid applause, Belle smiled and bowed. "You are most welcome, Mr. Scrooge."

"Now we print it," he said.

What Scrooge had in mind were handbills such as were used for all manner of announcements. He had arranged for immediate printing during a visit earlier in the afternoon, just before ordering the food. This was to the book printer and publisher Chamberlain, with whom Ebenezer had managed to place Belle's forthcoming book several weeks earlier.

Ebenezer had taken an instant liking to the firm's head, William, son of the late founder. The man's warmth and charm were extraordinary. He had a way of setting aside every other matter to center his attention on the person before him. Even as flinty a stone as Ebenezer found Chamberlain utterly winning and sincere. And yet conversation quickly revealed that he was also a canny man of business.

"This is quite a specialized book," Chamberlain had said of Belle's button-making treatise, "if we consider it a volume for instruction, yet it illuminates something that could not be more familiar nor closer to hand." He emphasized this by grasping one of his own jacket buttons. "From that perspective, it has universal relevance. The key, it seems to me, is to make it suddenly seem absurd that one is wearing items of complete mystery. The title might be along the lines of 'The Untold Story of Your Own Buttons.'"

"Exactly!" said Ebenezer, slapping Chamberlain's desk. Chamberlain comically started at the gunshot of a sound.

"I beg your pardon, sir," said Ebenezer.

"No, no, I could not be happier that we agree." Chamberlain punctuated this by slapping his desk with identical force. Ebenezer smiled.

"Will you please bring Miss Endicott around to me at your earliest opportunity?" said Chamberlain. Then he caught himself. "Oh, I do apologize. I've already forgotten the circumstance that led her to write the book. I will go to visit her. Is there any chance you could take me to their shop now?"

"This moment?"

"This very moment, sir."

"Certainly," said Scrooge, "if you are free."

"I am free."

Belle was delighted to meet Chamberlain, who could not have been more gallant in leaning over to greet Archie, particularly when the latter shocked everyone by reaching into Chamberlain's jacket pocket and snatching what he found there.

"Father!" cried Belle.

Chamberlain's momentary shock turned to boisterous laughter.

"Father!" Belle repeated as she presented her palm for Archie to return the item.

Chamberlain's laughter surged. Ebenezer had no idea what to think.

"Father," Belle growled, raising and replacing her hand to emphasize her command.

Like a boy, Archie abashedly relented and handed the ill-gotten good to Belle, who swiveled to tip it into Chamberlain's palm. He displayed it for Belle and Ebenezer with one word: "Father."

He said this of a toy soldier, a flat tin depiction of a redcoat with a black tricorner hat playing a drum. "He was in the infantry at the youngest possible age, playing the drum—my father was," said Chamberlain. "They called him The Little Drummer Boy, even when he made lieutenant, and he loved it. He's passed away now, and I carry this small token of him."

"How touching," Belle said.

"I do apologize for my laughter," Chamberlain said to her, "it's just that when you said 'Father!'—he had to suppress another chuckle—"it's exactly what was going through my mind when he was taken away!"

"I am the one who must apologize," said Belle. "Mr. Endicott is not himself."

"Do not worry yourself at all," said Chamberlain. He gamely held up the figurine. "I'm just glad that our fathers met."

"Pleased to meet you, Lieutenant Chamberlain," said Belle to the tin soldier with a curtsey. "And thank you for your service."

"Charmed, Miss Endicott," said Chamberlain, putting on a deep voice.

Ebenezer played along with a stiff bow. "Sir," he said to the toy.

"Mr. Scrooge," said Chamberlain. He used his bass tone for a final statement: "I shall now retreat." And back the toy went into his pocket.

When Ebenezer visited Chamberlain regarding handbill printing, he withheld the larger situation but quickly sketched his need for an immediate supply. Chamberlain, as was typical for him, listened intently and nodded in assurance.

"We have a hand press for just such purposes," he said, "and it is at your disposal. As soon as you have something to be typeset, bring it to me, and I'll put our chaps on it at once. You'll have all the handbills you like before you can sneeze."

"Thank you," said Ebenezer, rising and offering his hand. "I knew I could count on you."

"You are most welcome," said Chamberlain. "May I ask how the Endicotts are faring?"

"Quite well," said Ebenezer, "all things considered. I'm glad you asked. I told Belle that I would be visiting you about this, and she sends her regards."

"Ah! Please return the same."

"With pleasure."

Now with Belle's handwritten text in hand, Scrooge was about to return.

"I'm off again to Chamberlain," he told her.

"Give my greetings to his father this time," she said, smiling.

"If he produces the old soldier from his pocket," said Scrooge, "I certainly shall."

And he was off.

Less than an hour later, he was back with two

bundles of handbills. By then, the dinner hour had come, and hardly had Scrooge returned before his delivery of prepared food arrived, along with drinks and rented utensils. All was laid out in a buffet upon the front half of the day's stage after Usstin, Jonson and Sincello were escorted onto the floor by Marley. The employees happily left off their tasks and queued up to partake while the McHughs continued to perform. Some of the employees broke from the line to dance. Belle watched them with glee. Archie grinned and clapped.

Finally, the married musicians took a break for food, and Marley saw his three charges through the buffet. He directed them to spots along the wall and spoke with Scrooge as he kept an eye on them.

"How much longer now?" Marley said. He meant until the large Mercer order was complete.

"Three hours, perhaps a bit less."

"Everything seems to be on schedule."

"Yes," said Scrooge vaguely.

"And yet?" said Marley.

"And yet will any of this work? Is it pure lunacy?"

"Of course it is," said Marley. "And that is exactly why it will work. Mercer will never have seen the likes of this day."

"This evening. It is we who have never seen the likes of this day."

"It's been a long one for you."

Scrooge knew that he might be awake for a second consecutive night, but he shook his head. "I'll sleep when I'm dead."

"Not I," said Marley. "I'll be a busy haunt." He nodded toward the sales representatives, glumly murmuring amongst themselves. "I rather like tormenting poor souls who need a comeuppance." Here he affected a ghostly wail.

"You're a good man, Jacob Marley," said Scrooge, earnestly.

"Known for my forbearance," Marley returned drily. "Because I can be on your arse like four bears."

Scrooge spat out some of his drink.

"Shut up, you devil," said Scrooge.

"If you're not careful, you'll be known for benevolence," Marley continued, twirling his fork at the party-like atmosphere. Scrooge recognized Marley's pun on Belle's pet name for him.

He laughed again, and Belle looked over with a wondering smile. Scrooge waved, and she returned a nod.

"I still don't know what you see in her," said Marley. This was another dry comment. Scrooge had gathered through the day that Marley was impressed with Belle's poise and artistry.

"Beyond the fortune that she brings?" said Scrooge.

Marley grinned as he dug into his food.

seventy

The work concludes

The evening flowed on. The stage was cleared of the buffet and refilled with the sales scoundrels. Lamps were lit. The buttons in the order mounted. The employees labored on with fatigued smiles.

Finally, the work reached its end, and the last crate was closed. Marley once again escorted Usstin, Jonson and Sincello from their seats and stood with them at the wall. By now there was an easy routine for the floor managers to gather the workers at the stage. Ebenezer climbed up once again to address them.

"Thank you for your efforts," he said. "You have done everything I asked and more. I will keep you only briefly.

"As I have said, this is an extraordinary day. It has been leading to an unusual delivery: The cart with this order will be pulled by our three sales representatives rather than horses— "

The workers murmured at this new detail.

" —directly to the owner of the Mercer garment company at his home."

The murmuring increased, because Mercer had never been spoken of as a customer.

" —accompanied by a new version of a Christmas carol, written by my dear Belle Endicott— "

Many workers acknowledged Belle with smiles and light applause, even as they buzzed about this new information.

" —with the assistance of our talented musicians, Mr. and Mrs. McHugh."

The applause grew here, and the McHughs returned an appreciative instrumental flourish.

"Mr. James McHugh is my banker, Carlotta is his wife, and his supervisor, Mr. Jacob Marley, has honored me today by serving me as counsel and our salesmen as an attendant."

Marley also received applause, albeit lighter. Up went his two-finger salute.

"I am thankful for this help and particularly from all of you, each and every one. You have been patient through a long and, I can only assume, puzzling day.

"I am torn about asking the McHughs to present the new carol to you, because it has a somewhat troubling origin, and I do not want to disturb your rest after a trying day. But it seems only appropriate— "

The lift in his voice at the word would only have been

noticed by Marley.

" —and the lesser of two evils to have you hear it. And so you shall. The briefest of backgrounds is this: I learned only this morning that my sales representatives do not work for me. Or I should say, not for me alone. Mister Jonson and Mister Sincello did grow a roster of active customers. However, they have colluded with Mister Usstin to maintain phantom accounts. He brought me the names of tailor shops and garment makers who never actually bought from us. Those orders were from the company called Mercer— "

Whispering from the workers intensified here but thinned to stunned silence as Scrooge proceeded.

" —who some of you might know as producers of shirts and all manner of garments. When launching this business, I tried and failed to gain Mercer as a customer. Mr. Usstin succeeded by acting as their spy. I have been shocked to learn that he has been the eyes of Mercer inside our walls, able to report on every aspect of our operation. The strict Button of the Day system was useless against him. He was found out only because Mr. Marley recognized him from earlier misdeeds and compelled the truth. That is why Usstin, Jonson and Sincello have been kept in ready view through the day. I persuaded them that they would be better off casting their lots in the end with me than with Mercer, for this reason.

"I intend to turn aside this plot by Mercer, and anyone associated with that company runs the risk of gaining a black name. As surely as a pirate, I will board the vessel that is Mercer and advise the captain that I can sink his ship and him with it, unless he surrenders to me. My cannon is this song."

He raised one of the handbills. By then, Belle was fighting tears. Her Ben held the assembly spellbound.

From any other man, she thought, *the same plan and the same words would be ludicrous.* But Ebenezer's will was steel, his eyes coals, his tongue a sword. She had no doubt that he would accomplish his aim, not only his campaign against Mercer but also his broader goal to bestride London as a magnate.

"He's Androcles," she murmured. She didn't realize this had been in anyone's hearing until she found that Marley was whispering back to her.

"Except he will shove the thorn into the lion and then offer to pull it out."

"Will it work?" said Belle.

"Yes," said Marley, "if he isn't slashed to death on the spot."

Marley pardoned himself for his next duty— directing Usstin, Jonson and Sincello to distribute copies of the handbills. Scrooge invited McHugh and Carlotta to the stage.

"Feel free to sing along," Carlotta said. "It's to a tune you know." McHugh played, and she raised her silvery voice.

The workers joined in at once as they read the lyrics, and prickles ran across Scrooge's skin.

He found Belle. Through tears, she smiled at him and nodded. He could hardly wait to visit Mercer's doorstep.

seventy-one

A delegation embarks

Scrooge's group was fortified with a number of his workers. An initial volunteer had stepped forward, leading another to do the same. This made a lump rise in Scrooge's throat, and he was momentarily speechless.

"The more the better," Belle interjected on his behalf, and her blessing drew yet another volunteer.

"We will be glad to have you," Scrooge finally said. He announced a final thanks to the employees who filed out, many of them offering best wishes for the expedition.

With Archie enjoying the music so thoroughly, Belle insisted on going along with her father. "We'll put him in the cart," she said. And so they did. Devon assisted this, producing warm blankets to wrap Archie. He brought these with him after running the borrowed rocking chair back to its place.

"You dear, dear lad," Belle said. This time, she hugged him without even asking, and he glowed as brightly as before. He also fell in to carol.

Scrooge shook his hand. "Thank you, Master Rickman. Most helpful." Even as he said this, he lightly tugged the blankets so as to further conceal the cartons of buttons. The cart would appear to be in use only to transport an old man and his attendant, accompanying other carolers.

In all, they were a baker's dozen, with four of the employees accompanying Belle, Archie, James, Carlotta, Usstin, Jonson, Sincello, Scrooge and Marley. The bundles of handbills went into their own carton amid the blankets.

Scrooge explained the route to the group and estimated that they would travel just over thirty minutes. He knew the location of Mercer's home from his earlier effort to solicit the company's business. Then, he had been turned away from Mercer's door, but he had high hopes for this second foray. This caroling group would be his Trojan Horse.

"Let us go forth," said Scrooge. A hearty cheer arose.

Belle took Scrooge's hand as they set off and drew him close to whisper, "Bless us, every one."

seventy-two

Inside the mansion

Augustus Mercer disliked having Christmas carolers at his door, but his wife Marissa adored them, so each year as the holiday approached, the house staff was reminded to inform the family if carolers appeared, and Mercer would grudgingly accompany Marissa to the door.

On this evening, the footman reported to the butler, Mr. Harriger, that a large group had just arrived.

"How large?"

"A dozen, sir."

"Oh?"

"Yes, sir, or slightly more. Including musicians, sir—a fiddle and guitar. They're even carrying printed sheets—a list of songs, I imagine."

"Quite an organized group. Thank you, Henry."

She will be most pleased, Harriger thought as he moved to inform the Mercers. *He will not.* Such a contingent suggested a longer time at the door. Mrs. Mercer would think it inappropriate to quickly dismiss a group that represented such effort and care. Harriger foresaw Mr. Mercer's crestfallen expression upon learning the footman's news but he must share every detail so the master could marshal his constitution before reporting to duty, perhaps bolstering himself with a shot of brandy.

The family was yet at dinner. On his way into the

dining room, Harriger would direct the first footman to draw brandy and have it on hand to discreetly offer to Mr. Mercer as he trailed behind his bubbling spouse. Harriger would also whisper direction to the housekeeper that suitable coats, wrappings and gloves be brought to the front hallway. These could be provided to the Mercers to don sometime into the performance. It would reflect well on them to demonstrate this foresight and become equipped to stay longer. Their thoughtfulness would be commensurate with the size of the group.

Ah, thought Harriger, *he might be pleased at that.* If carolers had to come, at least a large group offered an opportunity to demonstrate noble bearing. Pleased after the fact, Harriger refined his thought. *In the moment, Master Mercer will simply endure.*

All of this was smooth fabric in his mind by the time he approached the dining room, but the first footman, Mr. Kendrick, just then exiting, immediately introduced a wrinkle, speaking before Harriger did.

"I'm afraid that Mrs. Mercer just fell ill, sir."

Harriger's nose was assaulted by a sickly stench as a house maid passed by holding away from herself a tray splashed with an unsightly puddle. The maid was struggling to quell a sour expression.

"You're a heroine, Victoria," Kendrick whispered after her.

"That I am," Victoria tossed back before fading from sight.

"She managed to place the tray just in time," Kendrick explained.

"I see," said Harriger. "Heroic indeed. How unfortunate for Mrs. Mercer. Is she at table yet?"

"Yes, sir, with another tray at hand if needed. She is taking care to remain still. Miss Docherty has been summoned. Mrs. Beverly is at Mrs. Mercer's side."

"Well done," Harriger said. Mrs. Beverly was the housekeeper, while Miss Docherty was Mrs. Mercer's lady's maid and personal companion. "I can see that you have matters well in hand."

"Thank you, sir. The staff has been utterly discreet," said Kendrick.

"I have no doubt. Would you please let Mr. Mercer know that I have a message for him?"

"Certainly, sir." He slipped away. It went without saying that Harriger refrained from entering so as to spare Mrs. Mercer yet another onlooker.

Just as Kendrick disappeared, Brigid Docherty swept past him, catching his eye with a wry expression, and he nodded to her. He halted a footman just about to enter the dining room and diverted him for the aforementioned shot of brandy.

Shortly, Mr. Mercer himself appeared.

"You missed the upheaval, Harriger," he said drily.

"So I understand, sir. I am sorry for Mrs. Mercer's discomfort."

"She's feeling a bit better. Brigid will escort her to bed."

"She has my best wishes, sir. I am sorry for the timing, because she will regret missing the visitors who just arrived."

"Visitors?"

"Christmas carolers, sir."

"Oh, of all the bloody hell." As Harriger stood attentively, he saw quick calculations flit beneath Mr. Mercer's creased brow.

"Pardon me, Harriger," said Mercer. He ducked back into the dining room entrance for a quick beckoning. A lively young woman joined him. This was Preshea Mercer, called Shea.

"Poor Mother," she said lightly to Mercer. Then

spotting the butler, she added, "You missed it, Mr. Harriger."

"It's a shame, Miss," said Harriger. "Your mother has my sympathy."

"Thank you. She needs it. She's mortified."

"It gets worse," said Mercer.

"Could it possibly?"

"We have carolers."

"Ho!" It was a laughing wince. "That is worse. Poor girl. She'll hate to miss them."

"She is not to know."

"Father!"

"Hush now."

"But you can't just send them away! She wouldn't hear of it."

"She won't hear of it. Not from her room."

"Father."

"I'm not going to send them away."

"Good."

"You will."

"I most certainly will not."

"Then go listen to them politely and make my apologies. I've got to tend my ailing wife."

"Oh, of all the poppycock. You're terrible."

"And you are only slightly less so. You are keeping the carolers waiting. Hurry now."

With an amused huff, Shea pivoted to leave.

"Off I go. Tend her tenderly."

"You know I shall."

" —from your study."

"I will hover as close as necessary."

"Like a demon on a shoulder."

"You flatter me, my dear."

"You owe me, Father," she called back in a stage whisper, already passing from view.

Kendrick appeared with the brandy. With an appreciative nod, Mercer tossed it back.

seventy-three

Carolers wait, and ...

Never announcing that she would do so, Carlotta assumed the role of choral leader, guiding the group through traditional favorites. For the time being, she avoided calling for the song of the hour, with its new lyrics.

After a number of rounds, Scrooge's anxiety mounted. So far, there had been no response from the stately Mercer home.

Belle beamed him a confident smile, made all the wider by Archie's contented rocking from the center of the music.

Gamely raising a boisterous bass, Marley cajoled Usstin, Jonson and Sincello into joining in, albeit halfheartedly. In time, Jonson seemed to forget himself and warm to the camaraderie, his voice climbing in volume and gaining an amusing punch. This might have had to do with nips that he had taken from a pocket flask.

Yet still the Mercer door remained fixed. Scrooge's stomach clenched. He was on the verge of stepping to the door knocker when at last, shadows of movement played on the walls within, and the door opened.

Out stepped a lovely young woman in a handsome woolen cloak. Two servants followed, each bearing a lantern. They hung these on hooks to the right and left, then retired inside and closed the door. Ebenezer and the other men doffed their hats. Belle deftly swiped Archie's flat cap from his head.

"Hallo now!" the old man said in protest. This coincided with the silence that had fallen at a gesture from Carlotta to suspend the performing. Belle hushed her father.

"Hello now, Miss," said Ebenezer, stepping forward, "and Merry Christmas."

"Hello and Merry Christmas to all of you," she returned, looking over everyone in the light of the lanterns. "What an impressive group." Her bright smile fell into a shape of surprise when her eyes reached the rear of the assembly.

"Teddy?" she said. "Is that you?"

"Happy Holidays, Shea," mumbled Usstin. Marley had noticed him trying to shrink into the shadows as soon as the young woman appeared, and he had jostled Usstin forward.

Teddy? thought many of those assembled. At the button factory, Usstin was known only as Theodore.

"Happy Holidays indeed," said Shea with the type of purr that reminds one that a cat has claws.

"I gather that you know Mr. Usstin," said Scrooge, replacing his hat.

"I do."

"Perhaps through the Mercer company?"

"Yes, our family business," Shea said. "But you and I have not met." She extended a hand. Scrooge took it.

"We have not. My name is Ebenezer Scrooge, and my company is one of your suppliers."

"My father's suppliers," she said. "I am Preshea Mercer. This is a kind gesture for your company to make." She slid her eyes back toward Usstin. "Though perhaps undiscriminating in whom you included." Then her brow wrinkled. "Wait, why is Teddy with you if he works for Mercer?"

"That's exactly the question I came to ask myself earlier today. I had thought that he worked for me, but I learned otherwise. He seems to have been active as an industrial spy."

"A spy? Teddy?" Shea cocked her head in consideration. "Ha, of course. He is just the type to hide his designs and hide them well. Has he done you damage?"

"To be honest, Miss, no. He has brought in significant revenue. But we learned that it was in service of harming our company. He feigned sales so that I would buy more equipment and extend myself financially. Then, when the orders disappeared from the phantom accounts, I would start to bleed to death, if you'll pardon my language."

"But there was revenue, you say? From these phantom sales? Teddy did hand over money for them?"

"He did. But he told me that it came from— "

"Forgive my interrupting, Mr. Scrooge. I can complete the thought in my mind, but I would rather not hear it spoken just now."

"As you wish, Miss."

"What do you supply to Mercer?"

"Buttons, Miss." Ebenezer handed her a packet of his products that included his card.

"Ah," she said, "I see. Then you have a factory?"

"Yes, Miss. Not quite a half-hour's walk from here. Or a cart roll, in this case." He indicated the vehicle. Shea looked there and nodded to Belle.

"How do you do, Miss?" said Shea.

"Very well, Miss Mercer," said Belle. "Thank you for asking. I am Belle Endicott. This is my father, Archibald." She playfully raised his cap as Archie would have done if more aware, and Shea's chin shifted in understanding. She returned a curtsey.

"I'm pleased to meet you, Mister and Miss Endicott."

"May I introduce you to the rest of our carolers, Miss Mercer?" said Scrooge.

"Please do."

Ebenezer worked through all of the names. Shea hopped in at the last, saying coolly, "And Teddy."

"Yes, Teddy, who brought us here," said Scrooge. "The cart holds his most recent fraudulent orders."

Shea raised her head for a better angle on the cart. Belle drew aside the blankets to reveal the cartons, and Devon moved in one of the group's own lanterns to illuminate them.

"So many buttons," said Shea, turning back to Ebenezer. "Were you going to leave them here?"

"Well, Miss, bringing the order with us is a manner of illustrating the situation. Taking them where they actually belong. I would like to discuss a resolution."

"I see. A sticky situation indeed."

"Quite."

"You have gone to a great deal of effort. Even bringing musicians." She swiveled to the McHughs. "You sound splendid, by the way."

"Thank you, Miss," said the McHughs.

"There's more to our preparation, Miss," said Ebenezer. He passed her a handbill.

Belle angled it toward one of the lanterns to read. As she did so, Ebenezer nodded to Carlotta, who strummed her guitar as a signal, and the group took up the song to the tune of *Good King Wenceslas*.

Ebenezer mouthed along as he watched Shea Mercer, whose attention remained fixed on the paper. Her expression was unreadable. The group moved through the verses with mounting gusto. Carlotta brought the number to a crisp, clean finish.

Shea looked off and remained thoughtful for long moments before she spoke.

"I must say, whatever the content, this is excellent wording. Very clever and artful."

"Thank you, Miss," said Belle, even as Ebenezer gestured to her with both hands.

"This is your composition, Miss Endicott?"

"Yes, Miss Mercer."

"Well done indeed." She turned back to Scrooge.

"This is a great deal to consider, Mr. Scrooge. I cannot speak for my father or the company. I am simply doing my best to grasp how you came to be here and with what concerns, so that I can help my father understand."

"And you have been most kind to do so, Miss. It feels fortunate that you greeted us."

"A happy accident borne of an unhappy circumstance, I am afraid. My mother adores caroling, but she is feeling poorly, and my father is attending her. Hence your performance only for me."

"I am sorry for your mother's distress, and I extend all best wishes. It has been a pleasure to speak with you."

"Thank you."

"I have no wish to sully a pleasant visit, but I must state as politely as I can that we are here because Mercer has launched an assault on my company, and I must withstand it as forcefully as I am able."

seventy-four

An ultimatum

"I do recognize and appreciate your courtesy, Mr. Scrooge. Please continue."

"Thank you, Miss. Simply put, I will retaliate against Mercer's reputation."

"Does Mercer have a reputation?"

"Well, that's just the thing, Miss. Most people are probably not aware of the Mercer name, even if they wear clothing made by the company. Perhaps Mercer has little or no reputation. But at least it does not have a poor reputation."

"A reputation for under-handed dealing, for instance."

"Precisely, Miss."

"And your song will foster that reputation."

"Songs can quickly become popular, Miss. They can spread like disease. Especially among the boisterous classes."

"The boisterous classes?"

"Those in taverns and pubs, Miss," interjected Marley. "I speak as a former tavern owner. Toughs who would have no call to sing a Christmas carol would seize on this one." He brandished his own copy of the handbill. "They'd find it mighty entertaining to make festive with sharp new words."

"I see," said Shea. "I am trying to be polite as well, Mr. Scrooge. It is not pleasant to think about my family's name being bandied about in taverns and on the streets."

"I don't want that, either, Miss. But the fact that this is worrisome to you shows you that this song is a weapon. It is a sword that I must wield. This is a battle I must fight. I cannot simply stand aside."

"And when will you commence this campaign, Mr. Scrooge?"

"Immediately, if I leave here without satisfaction."

"What would give you satisfaction?"

"I can answer without hesitation, Miss. I want to be a true supplier of Mercer. The current relationship is fraudulent and is being used for manipulation. I want it to be corrected and continued. My factory is the best way for your company to get buttons. I can promise that categorically. No source would be more reliable. No one would more closely examine Mercer's needs and meet them. Your company would never have worries related to buttons."

"You believe in your buttons, sir."

"I believe in my knowledge and ability to keep learning, Miss. I believe in the workers who I have hired. I believe in the processes that we have developed. I believe in our equipment. If all of that equates to believing in my buttons, then yes, I believe in my buttons. I will not have them taken from me without a fight."

Shea regarded him soberly. "You, Ebenezer Scrooge, are a black knight."

"I beg your pardon, Miss?"

"I do not mean the character in *Ivanhoe*." She waved away this connection to Walter Scott's wildly popular novel, recently published. "A most engaging figure, but one that my mother and I regret because the character stole a reference that she and I had long used for my father. It is our way of referring to him as a type of warrior with a gift for darkness."

A flush came over Ebenezer. He could not help feeling flattered, particularly since Miss Mercer was saying this in the presence of Belle.

"Business can be much like war, Mr. Scrooge. As you say, one must be prepared to fight. My mother and I have observed that warriors can sometimes get carried away. Battles can spin out of control with attacks and counter-attacks. This type of conflict suits my father. He thoroughly enjoys it. Mother has been an important civilizing influence. She has a way of drawing Father out about new developments in the company, and there are some that she will not tolerate. Sometimes she is able to turn aside my father, and sometimes she is not, or only by degrees. I can imagine what she would say about what you have told me. Mind you, I do not know whether he knows about your situation. He is the head of the Round Table, as it were. His brother knights in the company sometimes mount battles of their own, and he is completely or partially unaware. I will ask him about your particulars.

"At any rate, I have been in and around my father's skirmishes often enough to perceive that our own Black Knight"—she gestured toward the house—"has encountered another"—she gestured back to Ebenezer. "Your determination is evident, sir. I see that I must confer with my father at once and bring you an answer. Is that satisfactory?"

"Most satisfactory, Miss Mercer."

"Would you be so kind as to continue your caroling? I will ask the butler to invite out as many of the servants as might be able to enjoy your music."

"Delighted, Miss."

"Only, please— "

"No, Miss," Ebenezer said, intuiting her thought, "we will not sing the new carol."

"Thank you, Mister Scrooge. I will return as soon as possible, hopefully with my father."

seventy-five

Back inside the mansion

Oh, Reader. What caroling it was.

Many of the servants did emerge to take it in, and their expressions shone.

As careful as Shea Mercer was in her request to Harriger to notify the staff, and as discreet as she was in threading the halls to summon her father, her mother still somehow sensed the shift in the household.

Mrs. Mercer called to Shea as she passed by her room, and Shea looked in, nodding to Brigid Docherty as she entered.

"What is happening, Dear?" Mrs. Mercer said

"Whatever do you mean, Mother?"

"Don't even try that. I can tell. Something is happening."

"You are ill, Mother. That is the happening."

"I'm starting to rally, and I'll get up and find out myself if I have to."

"No, Mother, you need to rest."

"I need to know. Has there been an accident?"

"Other than yours in the dining room? No."

"Is there some kind of news?"

"News?"

"Darling, won't you just tell me? It's in the air. Whispers at the stable resound in the halls."

"I hear nothing. Do you?"

Her mother began to speak, but Shea waved her silent. They listened. There was nothing. And yet Mrs. Mercer blurted out, "Carolers!"

Shea rolled her eyes, giving up the jig.

"Because you're wearing your cloak! You've been outside."

Shea groaned inwardly at her mistake.

"You've kept them from me!"

"Guilty as charged, Mother."

"Your father had a hand in this, I'll wager." Mrs. Mercer threw back the blankets of her bed.

Shea peered sideways in feigned innocence.

"Scoundrels! Brigid, dress me at once. A housecoat and my cloak will do."

"Yes, Ma'am." Brigid knew better than to question her mistress, or worse yet, to so much as glance at Shea as if seeking her blessing.

"Just move slowly, won't you, Mother?"

"Are there many of them?"

"As many as we've ever seen visit. Over a dozen. Including musicians, no less."

"Musicians!" The news was as a tonic. Mrs. Mercer scurried to her dressing table.

"Slowly, Mother," reiterated Shea.

"And you weren't going to tell me."

"Shame on me."

"Shame on you!" Mrs. Mercer said, even as she turned to Brigid with a twinkle.

Smiling, Shea departed to give the bad news—all levels of it—to her father.

seventy-six

In the study

We will let this scene commence wordlessly. Mr. Mercer is comfortably ensconced with a book in a great chair in his study. Shea knocks and is admitted. She notes with a wry smile that what her father sets aside, along with a tumbler of Scotch, is none other than a copy of *Ivanhoe*. Out of necessity, Shea speaks quickly. Mr. Mercer gives a heavy slumping sigh at learning that Mrs. Mercer now knows of the carolers. He straightens as Shea rapidly summarizes everything she had heard from Ebenezer and imparts her impressions. This father and daughter have had many such conversations. Mr. Mercer absorbs everything impassively, inserting a few questions and statements, and soon the story is told. Shea passes him the packet of buttons, and he inspects them. She produces the handbill. He reads it, gives Shea a look, then reads it again. There is another round of questions and answers, concluding with another sigh, though it has a decidedly different tone. Mercer is quickening now. With a resolute heave from his chair, he stands and gives Shea a pat on the shoulder. He rings for his valet to fetch his apparel for the journey outdoors.

seventy-seven

The offer

After joining his wife and enduring a scolding, Mercer briefly remarked to her that he would be taking aside one or two of the carolers for a quick matter that he would explain later. Mrs. Mercer merely raised her eyebrows and nodded. Whatever curiosity she had about this was swallowed by her excitement about the caroling.

The master and mistress of the house made their way to the front entrance, where their coats and wraps were waiting. As they were helped into them, the servants who had been listening to the carolers streamed back inside, chatting happily, many of them tossing back thanks and holiday wishes. Mrs. Mercer beamed all the more as they passed.

Then all three Mercers emerged. The hats among the carolers again came off, and Archie once again blurted, "Hallo now!" Ebenezer reintroduced the group. Mrs. Mercer repeated each of the names with warmth and thanked them all for coming.

"I gather that you need to speak with me, Mr. Scrooge," said Mercer. "We'll want you too." He gestured to Usstin.

"And Mr. Marley," said Scrooge.

"As you wish," said Mercer. "My daughter will join us as well."

"Oh, not before hearing a carol, Dear," said Mrs. Mercer.

Her husband nearly managed to hide his irritation.

"No, of course not," he said.

" —or two," said Mrs. Mercer.

Her husband's equanimity was admirable. Shea slid her tongue into her cheek and caught Belle's eye. They exchanged quiet grins.

Soon enough, as the entertainment continued, the five parties named earlier stepped to the side of the vast entryway for their outdoor conference.

"My daughter has summarized everything for me," said Mercer. "We can resolve this quickly."

"How, sir?"

"I will send my associate Brewster to your factory tomorrow to take in everything for himself. Prepare a document of confidentiality for him, and he will sign it."

"Your intention, sir?"

"To get Brewster's recommendation on buying your company."

Scrooge would forever be grateful that he did not gasp at Mercer's statement. He noted as well that Marley did not. Shea did not. Only Usstin did.

"And if I do not want to sell, sir?"

"Why would you not want to?"

"Perhaps I want to continue running the company."

"Perhaps? Will you or won't you sell?"

Even Scrooge surprised himself with the speed of his realization.

"I will. Given an appropriate agreement."

"Then you will, if your company is sound. I know how to reach appropriate agreements."

"It is sound."

"Very well, then."

Only for a beat was Scrooge at a loss.

"Is that all for now, sir?" he said.

"Of course not."

"What else, sir?"

"Give me all of the handbills."

Another beat of calculation passed.

"At once, sir. Anything else?"

"Only that I'll want you"—he pointed to Usstin—"to remain when the others leave." Looking drawn, Usstin nodded.

"That is all, Mr. Scrooge," said Mercer.

"I have one remaining question, Mr. Mercer."

"Yes?"

"Where do you want your buttons?" He gestured to the cart.

Mercer grunted. "Brewster will direct you."

"Very well, sir." He drew his handbill from his pocket and offered it. Marley and Usstin did the same.

"You'll have the rest momentarily," said Scrooge.

With a scowl, Mercer took them.

"Thank you and Merry Christmas, sir," said Scrooge,

extending his hand.

Mercer gruffed back something very much like "Bah," but he did shake Scrooge's hand.

seventy-eight

A vision

On the way back toward the group, Marley drew Scrooge aside.

"Handing over all the handbills?"

"It's fine," said Scrooge. "It's in memory."

"Is it?"

"Yes, and not only mine." He nodded ahead of them. "I have Belle."

But even as Scrooge looked at her, his next step faltered. Belle was inside the cart, cradling Archie, whispering to him and smoothing his hair. With so little of them showing past the sides of the conveyance and in the darkness, lit only by the lanterns, and due to Archie's diminished state, Belle appeared to be cradling a small boy. It was a projection ahead, Scrooge knew. She would indeed mother a son. But somehow in that moment, he knew that Belle's son would not be his.

He came to a stop. Marley took another step before realizing his companion had halted, then he turned.

"Are you quite all right, Scrooge? Is something the matter?"

Scrooge felt the world fall away in a blur of muffled sound. He found himself rising, weightless, and twisting slowly like a scrap of paper burned in a bonfire and lifted on the swell of heat. The group of carolers was well below him now. He came even with the upper reaches of the Mercer mansion.

There was a touch on his sleeve, and then on his hand. He turned and saw—without ever having seen her, he still knew who it was—Lily Endicott. He had drifted to the vertical now, and he was suspended facing her.

He knows.

Scrooge could not have said whether Lily actually spoke—moved her mouth and lips to shape vibration from her throat—but her words in her voice came to him, followed by his own thought.

He knows. Father knows of my success.

Puzzlement wafted through him like a drop of ink dissolving in water. His father had not come directly. Lily had come and spoken for him. That meant something. The meaning was just out of reach. The answer was there, but veiled.

The answer. To Marley's question. Was waiting. For him to speak it.

Like air finding a tiny gap in a wall, Scrooge's vision streamed away, and he was in the instant of his own stalling and Marley's asking, "Is something the matter?"

"No, no," said Scrooge. "Just a bit light-headed."

"It's no wonder," said Marley. "What a day. Two days for you. And suddenly everything has changed."

"It has," said Scrooge. He realized that he had never ceased looking at Belle cradling Archie. He swung his eyes from them and found Marley, large and solid before him, looking as ever like a door knocker.

"Now I see the future," Scrooge said.

Marley helped him gather the handbills from each member of the group, even as they continued to perform carols. For the time being, their nods and smiles to the group served as explanation.

Marley handed his sheaf of copies to Scrooge and

took it upon himself to gather the remaining bundles of handbills from the cart. He fell in just behind Scrooge as he turned to relocate Mercer, who was just then resuming his place beside his wife.

"I'll take them, gentlemen," said a voice at his elbow. This proved to be an exceptionally tall and striking young man—the very model of a first footman—who clearly had been dispatched for this task. Scrooge and Marley transferred the papers, and the young man strode away with them.

Scrooge turned toward the stoop and found Shea looking at him. She lifted her chin in the subtlest of communications: *This went well. Away with you now.*

He touched his hat brim in salute, returned to the group with Marley, made his way to Carlotta and whispered to her. She nodded, smiled at the carolers and tilted her head to direct everyone to follow her away. With final waves, doffing of caps and and calls of "Merry Christmas" the delegation withdrew, singing and playing until out of hearing.

Scrooge spotted a well-lit space to halt, swiveled and said with arms outstretched, "It worked!"

The happy announcement brought cheers, hugs and handshakes, and everyone chattered and clattered their way back to the factory. All save Jonson and Sincello, who Scrooge bluntly dismissed.

"Come around tomorrow to settle your wages," he instructed them, "if you have the gall to collect any." They slunk away.

Archie stayed deep in sleep, and Belle remained wrapped about him. She beckoned Ebenezer to lean in for a kiss.

"What an accomplishment," she said. "No one else could have done this."

"No one else could have written the song."

"You had no one else to ask."

"True enough," he allowed.

"May you be happy, Ben," she said solemnly. "And proud."

He patted Archie's shoulder and straightened up knowing that he would never tell Belle of his vision of Lily.

seventy-nine

Fading hours

Archie died the very next day. The final distance that he traveled in this world was in Ebenezer's arms, from the cart to his bed, after Marley helped pull the cart to the Endicott's shop. Archie never woke from the sleep that he entered at the front of the Mercer home. Stirred by all that had happened, Belle sat up listening to his ragged inhalations, but then found herself waking to a room that was too quiet.

As the morning wore on, with Archie's breathing gradually slowing, Belle saw the end coming. She had a means of summoning Ebenezer—by imploring and paying a passer-by to take a note to the factory—but she would never have done so. Ebenezer expected Mercer's emissary to be at the factory for most of the day. She remained still and alone at Archie's bedside.

"Mama," she whispered at one point. Lily was cut off from her now, and Belle would not have sought her in spirit in any event. She would remain with her father to the last.

"Ben," she breathed somewhat later. Perhaps his

dealings at the factory would conclude, and he would arrive in time to sit with her as Archie faded.

"Miss Endicott?"

The voice drew her from communion with Archie's breaths. It flashed through her as a paradox—at once recognized and unrecognized.

"Miss Endicott?"

The voice came from out in the shop. She rose and stepped from Archie's room. Across from her was a young man leaning inside the entrance, holding the door partially open.

"I do apologize. I knocked, but you didn't hear," he said.

She could not place the young man, but she knew that she knew him.

"Miss Endicott?" the young man said again.

Moreover, she knew that she trusted him. Still she stood mute.

Cautiously, the young man entered and closed the door.

"Belle, what is it?"

There was still no response.

"Is it your father?"

She nodded, glancing back behind her.

"Shall I bring a doctor?"

She shook her head.

"Or Ebenezer?"

Another shake.

"Shall I sit with you?"

She nodded.

"All right then," he said softly.

The young man drew up a chair just outside of Archie's room, in view of Belle as she sat with her father. She intuited that he saw this as the best measure— preferable to entering into such an intimate space—and made silent agreement. It was not until then that she recognized her visitor and comforter.

It was William Chamberlain.

eighty

Why he appeared

Much swirled within Chamberlain as he sat with Belle. That was what had brought him there.

She had come to be on his mind constantly. At first, it had been the way that Ebenezer spoke of her when he initially proposed her manuscript for publishing. Ebenezer had presented a figure enveloped in wonder as well as admiration. It seemed that he was at a loss to fathom Belle as a person, much less his fiancée—as if she inhabited another world. Naturally, this was intriguing, but Chamberlain also gathered that Belle was strong and practical: She was an industrious craftsperson, ran her father's business, developed the concept of the secondary offering for Ebenezer's business—this becoming "Classic Buttons"—and conceived of the book project as her father's decline began to restrict her prospects. And it was indeed a sound idea. At the very least it was a worthy exercise for the sake of history, and it had potential to catch on as personalizing a momentous societal shift. The book presented a small opening into the large matter of industrialization, which was reshaping modern life like a scouring sandstorm.

Thus Chamberlain already had powerful curiosity when he got to meet Belle shortly after meeting her husband-to-be. By then, he was already flooded with fascination. Their brief exchange created a new layer of meaning to the sentimental totem of his father, the toy soldier. Because now Belle's father had held it, and Belle had rescued it for him. She had made something precious even more dear.

Then there had been her manuscript. It spoke to Chamberlain immediately, purely as an artifact of penmanship—or penwomanship, as he told himself. In Belle's steady lines, he saw clarity of thought, a grasp of detail and an intuitive ability to tell a story. He also came to believe that he could see echoes of her days. There were subtle shifts in wording and ink color that spoke to him of entering and exiting frequent interruptions. And when the precise writing came to wobble or drift—that must represent a point when she was on the last of a day's strength. There were many such wavering passages. She must routinely wring herself dry. It was nothing less than heroic.

My God, man, Chamberlain had come to say to himself, *you're falling in love with another man's fiancée. And you are her publisher. This is not appropriate.*

He immediately amended his thought. He was not falling in love with Belle. It was accomplished. He had already fallen.

The day came when Ebenezer made his urgent request for handbills. He had spoken in guarded terms, and naturally Chamberlain had not pried. When Ebenezer returned that afternoon as planned, Chamberlain made a point of averting his eyes from the folded paper that Ebenezer carried as he escorted him to the print shop. But as Ebenezer was handing the paper to one of the workers, it was caught in a gust of air from a door just then opened, and Chamberlain had reflexively followed it in flight. One of the lads seized it, but even the briefest glance showed Chamberlain Belle's handwriting, so familiar with it was he.

With a measure of guilt at this discovery, Chamberlain escorted Ebenezer back to his office for the brief wait until the printing was complete. He thanked the shop lads ahead of time for their quick work, and he whispered to the print shop manager that the typesetter was not to speak to anyone of whatever he composed from the handwriting. The man absorbed the cryptic directive solemnly, and he was trustworthy. Soon enough Scrooge was leaving with the printed bundles, as well as the original handwritten text, and Chamberlain waved away his request to send a bill.

"All best wishes," he said in farewell.

Soon he found himself at his desk looking out the window at the setting sun and pondering. So Ebenezer had enlisted Belle in what he gathered was a matter of some importance to the button business. There was always something brewing in the company— Chamberlain read this in Ebenezer's demeanor during each visit. The button-maker's cordiality poorly concealed the tension of a racehorse.

It must mean a financial difficulty. If so, that would extend to Belle as Ebenezer's wife. Or nearly his wife.

This would be on top of the decline of her father. Chamberlain did not have a sense for how Belle would bear up under mounting challenges. He knew that she was strong and had navigated the death of her mother at a young age. He knew from her manuscript that she had built endurance working beside her father from childhood. But her writing also revealed her soft and sensitive heart. Anyone might break if calamities mount.

Chamberlain felt a yearning to gauge Belle's spirit. His impulse was to visit her and inquire about her father. That would certainly be appropriate, since he had met Archie. Perhaps at the same time he would gain a broader sense of Belle's well-being. He would not seek details of the business situation. He merely cared for someone who had captured his heart, and it was not too early for him to explore an acceptable way to be a friend to both Belle and her husband. Or nearly her husband.

The day of the handbill printing was not the time to visit. He had to assume that Belle had been helping Ebenezer on his project. And since Ebenezer had needed the handbills immediately, the project would likely continue into the evening. And Belle would be tending Archie all the while. It would be a draining time for them. Hopefully, the night would be restful, and the morning would let them recover.

Then tomorrow afternoon, he thought. *Or perhaps late morning. Yes, I'll visit Classic Buttons just before noon.*

That was when he arrived and found the outer shop area empty but the front door unlocked. He ventured within and called to Belle in concern. Now he was sitting vigil with her.

He did not know what to think of Ebenezer's absence, and it was none of his business. But he was glad that he was on hand. Someone had to be.

eighty-one

Partnership talks

For the second consecutive night, Ebenezer did not sleep. For on the morrow he would sell his business.

It would take longer than a day, of course. There would be details to work out, and processes to navigate. But he knew the fitness of his operation. He had studied button manufacturing from its earliest days and had remained a diligent scholar even as his company launched and grew. He had a strong corps of suppliers, including alternate sources should an interruption arise. He knew every detail of his costs and had scratched for means of economy even as he carefully monitored the quality of his production. He had introduced innovations of his own, the secondary line of Classic Buttons among them, on which Belle's forthcoming book would build. Should the book become well-known, as it certainly had potential to do, it would burnish the entire experience that much more—this entire heady period of creation and nurturing. It was the richest time of his life. He hungered to do it again. And again and again forever. Give rise to an enterprise, infuse it with all of his effort and acumen, make it burst with value and reap ongoing rewards or a lofty purchase amount.

He had calculated the asking price for his business, and he knew that is what he would receive. It took no more than a handshake with Mercer and exchanging a few sentences with him to recognize a version of his future self. Mercer and his man Brewster would see what he saw, and they would invest as appropriate.

There was that word again, *appropriate*, the vital adjective and verb. Mercer would appropriate Scrooge's creation. In return, Scrooge would make Mercer's money his own, and that would be capital for his next endeavor. Sizable capital.

He and Marley discussed it as they hauled the cart back to the factory after leaving Archie and Belle at the button shop. She assured him that she and Archie would be fine, and she wished him a well-deserved rest.

"Let's do this again, Scrooge," said Marley.

"Let us?"

"All right, I came in only at the end this time, and I

lay no claim to the invention underlying your scheme. But I recognized it soon enough, and I daresay that you will need that in your career—a person of like mind but different perspective and capability. You have a creativity that I lack, and I have a touch of the common man that you lack. You are the mind, and I am the gut. And we are both men of will and a certain ... call it an aggressive ethic."

"Ethical aggression."

"Exactly. We'll play fair but with such force that it won't seem fair. They'll feel like taking us to court but will have no grounds."

"As straight and shocking as a lightning rod."

"See? There is your artistic bent now."

"So you propose a partnership?"

"I already have, you will recall. Marley and Scrooge."

"Scrooge and Marley is what I recall."

"Merely a test of your memory. Scrooge and Marley it is." He slowed his part of the cart-pulling, and Scrooge halted as well.

"Is it decided?" Marley said.

"It is."

They shook on it.

"Now then," said Marley as they took up the cart again, "what shall we do with all of the money that you'll receive?"

"That's obvious."

"Is it?"

"Certainly."

"Not to me."

"Why, we'll combine it with an equal amount of your money, of course."

"Ah, in retrospect, that is indeed obvious. And the first bill we shall split is for a lawyer to approve the articles of partnership that we draft."

"And then— "
"And then— "
"And then— "
They talked business for hours longer, like only death would them part.

eighty-two

The passing

Archie passed in the mid-afternoon. His breathing had become so quiet that Belle had to lean over him continuously, straining to hear him and to see the rise and fall of his breast. Finally, there was stillness and silence that did not end. Belle's hand on him was as on a folded bellows.

"Thank you, Father," she whispered. "Thank you, Archie."

She leaned back and put her head in her hands. Her weeping finally brought Chamberlain into the room. He gently put his hand on her shoulder.

"I'm sorry, Belle."

Her sobs deepened, and he remained still.

After a time, he carefully placed his handkerchief at her fingertips. "I'll be right here," he said. He stepped from the room and resumed his seat.

Belle sat facing Archie for the better part of an hour. Finally she turned toward Chamberlain. At once, he was on his feet.

"Thank you for being here," she said.

"It's a terrible loss."

"He was a good man, a good papa."

"I have no doubt."

"I don't know what to do."

"If you and Ebenezer need help, I will help you. I will tell you what I learned from my own father's passing."

"Please do. And Ben— Ebenezer— I don't know what he— I am sure that we would both welcome your help. I am sorry he was not here. I thought of summoning him earlier, but today at the factory—it's too much to explain, but I simply could not. Please do not think ill of him. It was my choice."

"Certainly not. I understand how complicated and interwoven matters can become."

"He may be along any moment."

"I will stay as long as you like, but if you prefer— "

"I am sure you understand."

"I do." He extended his hand. Belle nudged it aside and moved to embrace him.

"How kind you are," she said.

"How devoted you are," he said.

She drew back. "Thank you, William."

"You have all of my admiration and sympathy, Miss Endicott. I will see you soon."

And he left.

eighty-three

An inspection

Given the previous day, meetings gathering all employees in the button factory had become routine, if not expected. The makeshift stage was still in place in the morning, and Scrooge mounted it as soon as all the workers were present and assembled.

"Your efforts of yesterday proved of immense value," he said. "And our company is as strong and secure as it ever has been." Applause came from all corners.

"You have my sincere gratitude. You will note that Mr. Marley is here again today, but not to serve as an attendant. We have seen the last of the trio that he oversaw. New sales representatives shall replace them.

"In most respects, this will be a typical workday. However, you will once again see a visitor. Not unlike Mr. Marley, he has a particular interest in our enterprise, and I will be guiding him about the premises. Please answer any questions he might have for you but otherwise politely disregard him."

Mercer's man Brewster was just what Scrooge had expected, with one significant exception. The old gentleman was blind. Shea Mercer escorted him to the building, but he entered on his own and made his own way toward Scrooge's office, expertly arcing ahead of himself with his cane. There was a third member of their party, a gaunt young man who Scrooge surmised was an accountant.

Beyond a slight twitch of his eyebrows at his first sight of Brewster, Scrooge betrayed no surprise. Marley, on the other hand, uttered a soft curse. "Now I've seen everything," he said under his breath. His curt huff of a laugh indicated that his pun was accidental.

Shea Mercer introduced Brewster, who had a military bearing that made Scrooge suppose he had lost his sight on a battlefield, but there was no comment on his condition other than a request in his crisp, proper accent.

"In your responses, Mr. Scrooge, please set aside the fact that I cannot see. There is still plenty for me to perceive, and Miss Mercer is taking in all that I cannot. I will confer with her."

"Certainly, sir," said Scrooge.

Their companion, Mr. Boughry, was indeed an accountant. His sole interest was Scrooge's ledger, and he preferred to review the record alone in Scrooge's office.

"What a unique desk," Boughry commented.

"Thank you, sir. Feel free to use it."

With relish, Boughry did so.

Scrooge introduced Brewster to his floor managers and to various of the workers. Shea and Marley stood a few paces back, at times murmuring softly between themselves, but generally leaning in to hear the exchanges between Brewster and Scrooge. Now and again, Shea asked a question of her own, and she spoke to some of the workers.

The visit was methodical and thorough. Scrooge made sure that it covered every aspect that might be of interest. It concluded where it began, in his office. Mr. Boughry stepped down from Scrooge's desk.

"How are the books, Boughry?" asked Brewster.

"Meticulous and impressive."

"No questions?"

"No questions."

"As I suspected," said Brewster. "Mr. Scrooge, I think you know what you have here."

"I believe I do, Mr. Brewster."

"What would be your word for it?"

"Frankly, sir, a watch."

"Ah, yes. Tell me more."

"It is designed precisely to do what it does. With maximum efficiency and if I may say, elegance. Extensive study and thought is behind every element. It runs like a Swiss works."

"I tend to agree, sir."

"Tend to?"

"It is an imperfect watch."

"Is it? In what regard?"

"If we actually were, by some miracle, walking within a Swiss timepiece, there would be no sense of anything out of place. Everything would be precisely positioned."

"You found something out of place, sir?"

"I did. The second stove. It is excessive and steals space."

"Ah, yes. I must agree with you. It is interesting that you put your finger on that. I am removing it."

"It stood out to me as an afterthought," said Brewster. "Everything else is exactly and precisely placed, as you say. It either is or is not necessary for the warmth of the workers, and if it is, then you did not take that into consideration during the rest of your planning. It indicates a tardy shift in thinking. And based on what you say, you have judged it unnecessary, and your thinking has shifted back."

"That is accurate, sir."

"These things happen."

"Yes, sir. We live and learn."

"Having said this, I would leave the stove as it is."

"Oh?"

"For the new owner to address."

"Ah, yes." He smiled at Marley, who nodded back in satisfaction.

"I will recommend purchase of your enterprise to Mr. Mercer."

"I am pleased to hear that, sir. I will be proud to know that this operation is being put to good use."

"And you can move on to another endeavor. Keep living and learning."

"Yes, sir."

"Mercer has made many purchases and knows how to arrive at a satisfactory agreement."

"So Mr. Mercer indicated."

"Will you miss this place, Mr. Scrooge?" The question came from Shea Mercer.

Scrooge considered this for a moment.

"I expect that I will hold the memory. It has the distinction of being my first substantial commercial effort. But no, Miss Mercer, I am quite certain that I can leave unencumbered by sentimentality."

"Do you know what you will do next?"

Scrooge purposely did not look to Marley here.

"I have an idea."

"Something quite different?"

"Quite."

In time, Ebenezer was alone in his office. After bidding farewell to his visitors, he stood at his desk over his master ledger, sliding his hand over the page.

He closed his eyes, now as blind as Brewster.

This is what I would miss, he thought, *if I could not see. I could not bear life without these numbers.*

He closed the ledger and centered it perfectly on the slight incline of the desk. He stepped down and left the office, closing the door behind him. He mentioned to the floor manager that he would be gone the rest of the day.

"Very well, sir."

Very well, sir. The words echoed in his mind. *He knows things are very well.*

He?

He did not even know what the thought meant. His mind was not working.

Too long without sleep. He could not function a moment longer.

Had to, though. Had to go— He lost track of where he had thought of going.

Home. Simply had to go home.

Was supposed to do something, he thought as he

shambled along.

He made it to his flat, his mind sticking on what he ought to be doing.

He undressed and nearly swooned as he hung up his clothes.

He pulled up the cover, and it occurred to him what he had not done.

As he walked, he had not scowled. He didn't have the energy. This time. Must correct that.

He slept.

eighty-four

A fitful night

Belle washed Archie one final time and dressed him in his old wedding suit, which now gapped about his withered body.

Surely Ebenezer would arrive soon. There was the funeral to think about and plan. He was a planner. She was as well, but she craved his help. And his shoulder to lean on.

But he never came. For the second evening and long night, he did not come.

She feared that something had happened to him. Run down in the street by a carriage? Robbed and beaten and left for dead? Caught in one of his own machines and pulled apart? Disappointed during his meeting with the Mercer man and killed himself?

Eloped with Shea Mercer?

She curled up on her bed, fighting panic and filled with loneliness.

No father, no mother, no husband.

William Chamberlain. Her only friend that day.

The night was endless.

Scrooge awoke in pitch black realizing what he had not done.

Belle. Archie.

He sat up, swung his feet to the floor, halted. His head was swimming.

Wait, wait. Think.

It was the middle of the night. They would be sleeping. Archie had been exhausted by the entire doing. Happily exhausted, but drained nevertheless. He needed the sleep. Belle needed Archie to sleep as well. It was a respite for her.

He laid back down.

Unless something was wrong. But why was that any more likely than any other night?

Because Archie was dying, of course. Still. It would not be tonight. Would it?

Regardless, he had not told Belle the good news. He had not even thought to share it with her.

His ledger. He stood over it blind and thought it the only thing he would miss seeing.

Lily. He had seen her.

Belle's child. Not his child.

Belle. She must sleep.

Sleep. He must sleep.

He slept.

Belle sat up in lamp light, her mourning dress on her lap. It needed only a bit of sewing—the hemming of the collar, which she had purposely left undone until she would actually need to wear the garment. And the placement of a black ribbon over the heart. She had worked on it slowly and meditatively for weeks as Archie declined, naturally only while he was asleep, alternating between this work and drafting the book. Each task had acquainted her with what was coming. Here it was.

She hemmed the collar keeping careful attention on the stitches, resisting the tug toward the portal that would lead to Lily. Or always had led. It was closed off now. Was it? Yes, it was. She took a breath and set aside her wavering. She would never see her parents again.

She moved on to the ribbon for her breast. She cut an extra piece to sew a hanger for the shop door. This was her life now—signaling her loss.

She finished the ribbon sewing as well and sat with the dress. Not thinking, not moving. Nothing more to do. Only wait for the sun to rise.

It was still dark when Ebenezer started awake once more. He could not have slept long in this second stint. He would not try again.

He lay still briefly, again thinking of Belle. What came to him was the distance between them. It was only the distance of city blocks, short to walk, and yet he felt the size of it like a wall stretching from earth to sky. Belle felt a piece with that gigantic structure. She would always be on the other side.

No, of course she would not. He repelled this notion even as he threw off his blankets. They would be on the same side, side by side, man and wife.

He stood. It was time for a thorough washing and careful dressing. He would stroll to Belle and Archie's home if only to see the darkened window and stand outside thinking of her from much less distance.

He knows.

It was Lily's voice. Belle snapped awake at the sound of it, her heart racing.

She had nodded off in her chair. She gasped for breath and gulped in air.

He knows.

Lily's voice faded, but the thought remained.

"Mother?"

There was no answer.

He knows. Belle did and did not know what it meant. It reminded her of the previous day, when she had seen Chamberlain and yet not recognized him.

She shook her head. Enough of this. She rose to wash and put on her new dress.

The sky was just starting to gray.

The gray was softening as Ebenezer stepped out onto the street. He scowled as he walked, purely to reinforce his nascent habit. There was no one to receive his dark demeanor.

A smile edged into his frown as he thought of Marley. What would he make of this glowering practice? He had seen it the other day but of course had not known that Scrooge now intended it for every walk. It would come up in conversation at some point. He felt certain that he and Marley were destined to discuss every last thing.

And Belle. What would she make of it? His frown deepened. She would not like it. Just as she had not liked the workers being cold and just as she would not like his removing the second stove.

Wait, he would not remove the second stove. Brewster had advised him to leave it be. So he would turn over his factory, perfect in every way except for that addition by Belle. No, he could not lay the blame on her. He had succumbed. No more of that. He would hear her suggestions and make them his own—or not.

His walk was quick and rhythmic now. The sleep had done him good, and now this brisk pace was. He felt more himself.

He turned the corner to Belle's street and was surprised—dismayed and delighted in equal measure—to find the soft glow of lamplight at the shop.

He drew up and peered cautiously through the window.

Oh no, no, no.

Belle was sitting perfectly still in mourning dress.

Even as Ebenezer was about to rap lightly on the door, she rose and crossed to open it.

She burrowed into him.

"Belle, my dear Belle," he said. "I'm so very sorry."

"I know, I know."

He had the sense to simply stay still holding her. It seemed that all she wanted was to remain fixed in place.

She was not crying. He supposed that must mean she had already wept long and hard and had run out of tears.

She finally eased back and gave him a thin smile, patting his chest. He removed his hat.

"When did— "

"In the afternoon."

"Oh, Belle. I beg your pardon. There was nothing left of me after yesterday and the day before. After all was done at the factory, I stumbled home only half alive and fell into bed."

"No, I know, I know. How did it go?"

"It's good, very good. But let's wait on that. Tell me how it was for you. I'm so sorry I wasn't here."

"It was peaceful. Father never woke up after you put him into bed. You carried him to his final resting place, Ebenezer."

He closed his eyes and sighed. "I left you alone."

"I did not feel alone. It's over now. Please come and see him."

They stood over Archie. Ebenezer carefully reached out and ran his finger on the edge of Archie's lapel. Belle did the same on the other lapel.

"Father made this suit for his wedding, did I ever tell you?"

"Yes, I recall. Masterful." He addressed the man directly. "You were good to me, Archie. Rest in peace."

They returned to the outer room. The sun was pinking now.

"Could we go for a walk?" said Belle. "He'll be all right."

eighty-five

The walk

"Will you tell me now how it went at the factory yesterday?"

"Well, I must say, it could not have gone better. Mercer's representative Brewster liked what he—oh, I was going to say what he saw, but—Belle, he was blind."

"Blind."

"Blind, my dear. He used a cane. He arrived with Shea Mercer, and— "

"Oh, she came as well?"

"Yes, darling. And I have a thought about that in a bit, but— "

"Oh, do tell me now. I'm curious. She is a striking young woman."

"Ah, well. I thought that it was strange that she came along."

"Oh?"

"Yes, it would seem too small a matter, don't you think?"

"Too small? Reviewing a company to purchase?"

"Well, it was too small for Mercer himself. I do find that understandable. His company is massive, and relative to that, even the purchase of another business is something that he would delegate. I suppose I mean that it seemed unnecessary for Miss Mercer in particular to be along. Brewster did need someone to transport him to the company, but an accountant came as well, and he could have delivered him. He stayed in my office with the ledger, but Mr. Brewster was perfectly comfortable touring the factory with his cane. He didn't need to be held by the arm."

"Was Miss Mercer serving as another set of eyes? Well, not another set—serving as his eyes?"

"Brewster did make reference to that, but he never made use of her eyes. Any questions he had went to me. He merely conferred with the accountant, Boughry, as to the fitness of the figures, and he was satisfied."

"What did the accountant say?"

"His exact words were 'Meticulous and impressive.'"

"Sounds like you, Ben."

He acknowledged this with an inclination of his

head. "To be honest, it seemed as if Mr. Brewster truly could see everything that he needed to see. It was as if he took in everything simply by passing through it."

Belle fell quiet for a step, then two, then spoke.

"Sometimes it is the opposite. We move along but do not see."

"Yes, I suppose."

"There is something I have started to see."

"Oh?"

"I will tell you, but let me ask you first: I gather from everything you have said that you will sell the company?"

"Yes, Darling, I fully expect to. Brewster repeated what I heard from Mercer himself—that we will arrive at a suitable agreement. And since that cannot happen without the price that I have in mind—and have spoken about with Marley, with his confirmation—well, if Mercer has completed many acquisitions, and I'm sure that he has, then I cannot be far off the mark. I declare it definite."

"Congratulations, Dearest. You must be very happy."

"It is pleasing, I must say. It is good for us."

She took his hand and drew him to a halt.

"It is good for you," she said.

"For us."

"Ben, I must tell you what I have been thinking." Tears were in her eyes.

"Belle, what— "

"My heart is breaking. It broke only yesterday, and it is breaking again. The fragments are powder."

She removed her engagement ring. Ebenezer stood shocked.

"Listen to me, Ben. This is a little thing. You will have a long life. I am a small part of that, and I will grow smaller in your memory all the time. You will bestride London, just as you have said. If your magnificent accomplishments will cheer you and comfort you, as I would have tried to do, I will have nothing to grieve."

"Belle, no. No. Please. Any accomplishments are nothing beside you."

"That is not so. You walk with them as with another woman."

"How can you say this?"

"A woman with hair of gold."

"I don't understand." He was bewildered. Did she actually mean another woman? Did she mean Shea Mercer? She could not possibly. He had only just met her. Should he not even have mentioned her? She did not have golden hair.

"I do not mean another woman, Ben," she said, as if reading his mind. "I know there is no other. I did not mean hair of gold. I meant gold."

"But— "

"I will not fight to tear you away from gold."

"Belle, you overstate the matter. I do not chase gold for the sake of gold. We live in a hard world. It sneers at the poor and condemns the prosperous. If I will be spurned either way, let it be for the latter."

"This is not about the world, nor ultimately about money. It is about your fear."

"My fear!"

"I have spoken to you about this. You cannot put yourself beyond reach of your own reproach. Nothing is enough. All of your hope is in gain. Not in me, not in our family."

"My hope is in security. For us, for our family. I am not changed toward you."

She shook her head.

"Am I?"

"I think you have lived a lifetime without me since our engagement. It was forever ago that we were both poor and content to be so, until, in good season, we could improve our worldly fortune by our patient industry. You are changed. When you proposed, you were another man."

"Or a boy, if it was all this time ago."

"You know this," she said.

"Know what?"

"That you were not then who you are now. I am still who I was then. We used to happily plan the same life. Now that life would make you miserable. I have spent more time imagining our future than you might fathom, and it was pleasant until I realized that you did not want to be there with me. I release you."

"Have I ever sought release?"

"In words, no, never."

"How then?"

"In a changed nature. In an altered spirit. By breathing different air and orienting toward a different hope. My love ceased to have value for you."

"It has not!"

"Look at me, Ben." She was mild even as she held his gaze. "If we met today, would you try to win me?"

The blasted second stove flashed through this mind, and he faltered.

"No, you wouldn't."

"You only think that."

"I would gladly think otherwise if I could, heaven knows. But the truth overpowers me. If there were nothing between us today, tomorrow, yesterday, I cannot believe that you would encumber yourself with a poor girl not as intent on securing prosperity as you are. If you did temporarily question your desire for gain and choose me, I know you would come to regret it."

"You can't know that."

"I do, Ben, and I release you. With a full heart, for the

love of him you once were."

"Belle, please— "

"I had to tell you all of this now, while you are soaring in your ambition and have triumphed so magnificently, because that will help counteract any disappointment that you feel. I tell you again: I am filled with pride in you. I am happy for your success. I will not take advantage of your rise in fortune to aid with Father's burial. I would never let you help me with that and then immediately after share these thoughts with you. It is better to part now."

He was about to speak, but she looked away and resumed.

"Perhaps you will—the memory of what is past half makes me hope you will—have pain in this. But if so, it will be a very, very brief time, and you will dismiss the recollection, gladly, as an unprofitable dream, and be happy that you awoke. May you be happy in the life you have chosen."

She laid a hand on his sleeve.

"Please let me walk back alone. The sun has risen, and I am safe. I know that we will need to speak further, about the disposition of the shop and the publishing of the book. I will greet you warmly whenever I see you. Let us go forward in cooperation and affection. I do love you, Ebenezer Scrooge, and I always will. Always."

She left him. He stood watching her departure until she disappeared from sight and somewhat longer.

He found something in his hand. It was her ring.

eighty-six

Forever after

In years to come, he could not say what became of that ring, nor of his ring that matched it. He supposed that he simply put them away and let himself lose track, sinking them into a pool of forgetfulness. It was inconceivably profligate of him. Their selling price was one of the few sums that he ever failed to pursue. Nor did he choose to retain either ring as a reminder of what he once had but lost.

What he did keep was the red button. He kept me.

Scrooge would sit evenings in the dark holding his gaze on me as I hung in my place. Sometimes he would drift off to sleep this way, slumped into the corner of his tall, stiff, upholstered chair. Sometimes he would draw close to me but purposely look away, placing one hand on the mantel as he stood facing the waning fire. Sometimes he would enter the chamber and immediately undrape my ribbon from its hook and pace about, furling and unfurling me or running both the ribbon and me in and around his fingers.

There were countless variations, some subtle, some dramatic, that amounted to the same arrangement: Scrooge alone with me. I came to abide in his pocket at all times when he went out. Over the decades, as much as he handled me, any alteration was imperceptible. I was sturdily made.

What an odd existence. This is not the end for which I was fashioned. Though since this is what did occur, it has proven to be exactly my purpose—to serve as a reminder of and portal to what was unfulfilled. I was initially made to fasten fabric, and I never have. The only thread ever drawn through me is the cord that attaches me to Scrooge. I have held together not the man's clothing but the man himself. I helped him keep from flying apart. It might not be too much to say that I bound him to the earth, because he often thought about his eventual departure and even wished for it to hasten. But I had been touched by one who touched him, and that appeared to be enough for him to persist in living, such as he did.

Approprio. Approprio. Approprio. It has been a refrain all these years. Scrooge sometimes murmured the word all through the evening and drifted off with it on his lips. "To make one's own." He voiced the definition often enough as well. And the alternate definition: "Right and proper."

Nothing demonstrates the conviction that all is not right and proper like endless insistence that it is. He willed his fate to be correct, his destiny fitting, but that never made it so.

We were the same, Scrooge and I. What he did was not why he was made. He dwelled alone and amassed an unspent fortune. The very existence of people in groups belied and rebuked his solitude. In an alternate reality, his place would have been among others. Just as an alternate reality would have placed me in a line of buttons. Both of us were cut off from our fellows.

After the Classic Buttons shop was sold, Scrooge never laid eyes on Belle again, not up close. He could not bear to. He went out of his way to ensure that he would never see her, even accidentally. He ensured it with spies.

These operatives were his one expense that could have been deemed unnecessary. From the cage of his spirit, Scrooge sent envoys to roam the earth. He continued to think of this as journalism for his sole consumption. He paid his correspondents in cash so as to leave no evidence and purposely never employed any informant more than once. It was as if each agent was the only and the last.

Save Marley, no one ever perceived this practice, and Marley knew only because of his sharp observation. Scrooge never mentioned Belle to him, much less the outlandish way that he monitored her. And Marley, in turn, never commented. As freely as he and Scrooge discussed all other matters, he left this area alone. It was clear to him that Scrooge wanted to be a sort of angel hovering above Belle and her family.

Yes, her family. She married William Chamberlain, as you will have surmised. They found a supremely satisfying and comfortable match, fruitful in children and all other blessings. Scrooge's part in this was utterly unseen and uninvolved. He knew every development— every gain and loss, every illness, misfortune or stroke of serendipity. His spies told him.

If he reserved his vast wealth for anything, it was to move the hand of fate on behalf of Belle's family. Or to be poised to do so. The fact is, he never had to. The family received all manner of good fortune. Each member remained as healthy as could be. Chamberlain was an exceedingly wise and prosperous figure of business. Belle's books—she wrote several more under her own name—had modest but consistent sales.

It is worth noting that Scrooge helped ensure the success of Belle's first book—Archie's ghostwritten, posthumous memoir of cottage button-making. A condition of the sale of Scrooge's company to Mercer was the conglomerate's purchase of cases upon cases of the book for distribution to newspapers and the new institutions called libraries. This clause was inserted after Scrooge convinced Shea Mercer of the wisdom of continuing to offer a secondary line of nostalgic buttons. He impressed upon her that the Endicotts' book was a means of sustaining the vanishing craft, if only for Mercer's unique purpose, because it taught the fundamentals of button-making by hand. Shea had grown up among finer things and expensive fashion, and she saw that her family's company would always need capabilities that had started to be known as "boutique," a borrowing from French for "small shop."

"I read your fiancée's manuscript," Shea reported to Scrooge during the negotiations.

"Her late father's, you mean," Scrooge mildly corrected.

"Yes, of course," Shea said knowingly. "My deepest sympathy."

Scrooge nodded in acceptance.

"How fortunate that he lived to see the text completed, if not published."

"Very."

"I agree with you that the book is well worth Mercer's support and to our advantage. To ensure ourselves of even a small corps of bygone artisans, we will need a way to educate them."

"There is also the matter of reputation."

"Oh?"

"As we discussed briefly outside your home."

"Oh, yes. In regard to Mercer's having no reputation."

"But that one might be created."

"For better or worse."

"Precisely. And it seems prudent to me not to leave this to chance or the actions of others."

"You are talking about cultivating a reputation."

"I am. Even in these early days of high-volume manufacturing, it is apparent that many goods will cease to be unique. If I duplicate a particular factory with particular machines, I can make the same goods. The only advantage I will have is if my customers prefer to buy from me or from my company personally—as it were, as if my company were a person with a unique character."

"Fascinating. I see that you have given this much thought."

"I think much about many things, Miss Mercer, but yes, my favorite vein of rumination is business, and another is innovation, and the two intersect. There will be countless innovations in business. We are living in a time of great and rapid change, and the only way to prosper will be to change actively rather than have change forced upon us. I am fond of thinking that companies need to learn to become the companies that would put them out of business—to attack themselves, as it were, before being attacked."

"Ah, The Black Knight speaks."

"As you might say."

"That is your own reputation, whether or not you actively cultivated it."

Scrooge gave another nod of acknowledgment.

"Now as for the reputation that Mercer might cultivate?" Shea asked.

"If Mercer wished to be seen as a particular person," said Scrooge, "I would suggest a beneficent aunt."

"Really?" said Shea, with a surprised laugh.

"I see that strikes you oddly."

"Quite."

"Because?"

"Well, I had never thought about this before, but I see now that I associate the Mercer company with my father, and as you have seen, though you've spent only minutes with him, he is anything but a beneficent aunt. A truculent uncle, certainly."

"Very well, then. That illustrates my thinking indirectly. Because in countless ways, the company will make decisions in keeping with that unarticulated identity. However faintly, the company will take on an aggressive and combative character."

Shea Mercer was up and pacing now, grasping Scrooge's thought. "An accidental reputation, expressed unconsciously. Puny berries left to grow wild."

"The opposite of cultivation, yes," said Scrooge, whose reading had included tomes on plant husbandry and agricultural breeding.

"Why a beneficent aunt?"

"Because an aunt can provide clothing without offending the mother who did not make it herself."

Shea was stunned. "I think you might be a genius, Mr. Scrooge."

"Far from it. As I've said, I simply enjoy thinking about business."

"How does Miss— pardon me, Mister Endicott's book relate to Mercer's desired reputation?"

"You will be making buttons outside of the home, but you have no wish to offend home button-makers or the many who have affection for them and for bygone times in general. In fact, you continue to employ them and even celebrate them by supporting a book about home button-making written by a home button-maker."

"How will the public know that we supported the book?"

"You purposely drop the word here and there. Not with any public announcements, but through your sales representatives, who sing the praises of the book. That is the kind of generosity and humanity that shop owners repeat on their own accord."

"Word of mouth."

"Good word of mouth."

Shea leaned back and regarded him. "I still say you are a genius, Mr. Scrooge."

"That is all well and good, Miss Mercer— "

"Shea, please."

"Shea. But that is not the reputation that I will cultivate."

"Oh, will you nurture my other designation? The Black Knight."

"Not quite. I do want to present a certain darkness of demeanor, however."

"What is your intention, then?"

Scrooge spread his hands as if conjuring a sign in the air. "Miser."

"Miser."

"Miser. I am a firm believer in minimizing costs in every area that is not crucial, to allow investment in those few areas that are. I want everyone to think that I spend money on nothing, to disguise the fact that I spend heavily where it is crucial. I want competitors to dismiss me as unsophisticated and scornful of every expense, rather than opposed only to every nonessential expense. My stinginess will encourage them to outstrip me in every area. They will indiscriminately overfeed the pets that are their businesses, while mine remain lean and ravenous, and I will tear them asunder. By the time they realize that they have misjudged me, it will be too late."

"Thus one woman's Black Knight is another man's miser."

He gave a final nod of acceptance.

He left that meeting buoyed in spirit, but with every step he sunk back into despondence. He was no genius, nor Black Knight, or if so not at the moment. He was simply a man spurned.

But no, that thought was not fair to Belle. She had judged him, and he had faith in her perception. She understood him. In her own words, she admired him and believed in him like no one ever had or ever would again, of that he felt certain. He did not doubt her love, albeit, as she had said, for the man he once was. Or perhaps who she had thought he was.

But even if she loved him, she saw that she could not build a life with him, any more than she could yoke herself to a man whose true calling was the priesthood. He shook his head at the comparison, but was it not— there was the word again—appropriate? His only union could be with the kingdom of commerce. Everything and everyone would always come second to making property his own.

The only route he could see was to make Belle his own in an unorthodox fashion. From afar, he would would make Belle's security his life's mission. He would protect what was most dear to her. This is what made him her hovering angel.

But here, too, was unceasing frustration, though for the best of reasons. He could only hope that Belle would never need him, and she never did. As described, the family was never unduly pressed. The worst that befell them was a kitchen fire that took two rooms of their home, but these were quickly rebuilt. Scrooge knew of this at once, of course, and he was relieved to learn that there were no injuries. He was prepared to anonymously provide Belle and William a new home, a new neighborhood, an entire estate if they liked. But they recovered rather easily. This cheered and devastated him. He ached to serve Belle, but he must be glad that she did not require his service.

Their one contact over the years came when Scrooge's sister died. He was past sixty by then, and Fan past fifty. Shortly after the burial, an envelope arrived from the home of Mr. and Mrs. William Chamberlain. Scrooge let a week pass before opening it, and in that time all manner of speculation ran through his head. In the end, he opened the envelope carefully and impassively read the note enclosed.

Please accept our sympathy on the loss of
your sister. May you find comfort in the
memory of your family attachment.

Mr. and Mrs. William Chamberlain

That was all. The note speared Scrooge to the center of his soul, for there was no mistaking her handwriting. Through the following months, he imagined every minute detail of the news reaching Belle and her forming thought of him. He dreamed of her gathering her writing materials, composing the note and sending it off. The pain of this, following on his melancholy for his dear Fan, was crushing.

It brought memory of how he had attended Archie Endicott's funeral from afar. He had employed a spy even for this. The boy brought him word of the arrangements, and through him he learned to the moment when Belle was leaving for the cemetery. He knew the ground from having visited Lily's grave, and he devised a way to look on without being seen.

Archie meant something to him. It was the man's trade that drew him to the shop. Without that he never would have met Belle, and he never would have had even the opportunity for happiness, obstructed though it proved to be. Moreover, like Fezziwig, Archie had treated him like a son. Scrooge had to find a way to be on hand for Archie's committal and to recognize his reunion with Lily.

He stayed at a distance out of view and slipped away before the ceremony concluded. In the dead of that night, he returned and drew close to the plots and regarded the matched tombstones. The moon gave enough light for him to see that each held a button.

It occurred to him that he had never seen his father's headstone. He knew that Percival Scrooge had one, because he had sent Fan money for it. It also occurred to him that if he went there, he would have nothing to leave, no piece of himself. The only token that he might deposit would be a crass metal coin. Nothing as appropriate as a button.

The End

An invitation from
Keith Eldred to join the
THIS IS RED
Reader's Club

THIS IS RED is a collection of 20 Christmas books, all published in 2020. I email once a month about new releases, special offers and other updates on the THIS IS RED project. When you subscribe to the mailing list, I'll send you these FOUR BOOKS for FREE:

1. My standalone novella, *Elfred*
2. Book 1 of 4 in my short story collection, *Down to Earth*
3. Book 1 (*Santa*) and Book 2 (*Sandra Claus*) in my 10-book series of poetry and other short pieces, *North Pole Haiku*

Just sign up at www.thisis.red

See more about
THIS IS RED
on the next page

About the Author
and THIS IS RED

Keith Eldred created the THIS IS RED project with his wife Janet, a public library director diagnosed with early-stage dementia. With Janet's condition making every day precious, they decided to publish 20 Christmas books in 2020, the year of their 30th anniversary. All profits go to Janet's work home, the Hollidaysburg Area Public Library.

For more information:
www.thisis.red
www.hollidaysburglibrary.org
red@thisis.red
@thisisdotred